MW00575750

WHOLE

DEREK UPDEGRAFF

WHOLE

A NOVEL

SL/NT
BOOKS

WHOLE
A Novel

Copyright © 2024 Derek Updegraff. All rights reserved. Except for brief quotations in critical publications or reviews, no part of this book may be reproduced in any manner without prior written permission from the publisher. Write: Permissions, Slant Books, P.O. Box 60295, Seattle, WA 98160.

Slant Books
P.O. Box 60295
Seattle, WA 98160

www.slantbooks.org

Cataloguing-in-Publication data:

Names: Updegraff, Derek.

Title: Whole: a novel / Derek Updegraff.

Description: Seattle, WA: Slant Books, 2024

Identifiers: ISBN 978-1-63982-169-3 (hardcover) | ISBN 978-1-63982-168-6 (paperback) | ISBN 978-1-63982-170-9 (ebook)

Subjects: LCSH: American fiction | California--Fiction | Homeless persons--Fiction | Mental illness--Fiction

For Elizabeth

I

A Person and His Angel

ONCE IT HAPPENED that a person could see his angel. At first it was odd for the person, but he grew to love the praise he received for doing basic things. When the person poured his coffee, the angel smiled and gave him a thumbs-up, as if to say, Perfect pour, even though he'd actually spilled a little. And when the person rinsed out his mug and set it upside-down on the drying rack, he looked to his angel for recognition, and sure enough his angel shot over another smile and thumbs-up combo, suggesting that in the history of this world not many maneuvers had been performed with comparable grace. And so it went. Driving steadily to work. Sitting upright in his chair like a good person. Smiling to others. Working diligently, whether with computer or pen or phone or just in his mind. Talking to others without a bicker, with zero hint of *Oh, I envy you*. Reading the newspaper while on break or at home. Relieving himself at work or at home. Sitting on the couch just right. Chewing his food just right. These accomplishments prompted thumbs-up after thumbs-up, head-nod after head-nod, smile and smile and smile and smile. While sleeping, the person would sometimes wake, and he'd squint until he could see the angel alert in his chair. And there was the double thumbs-up with encouraging nod. Really amazing job sleeping, he'd gesture. The best, the best I've seen, he'd gesture. And then, as he always did, the person would whisper to himself, "I'm so very good at living. I'm so very good at living."

1

I HIT A HOMELESS MAN today. First day of spring, which is supposed to be about rejuvenation and coupling up. You know, the reverdie tradition, except out here in the desert. So it's the first morning of spring, and I hit a homeless man. Rammed right into the back of his bike. It's a miracle he's alive, Ronnie, the homeless guy I hit, since my car mangled his bike after he'd been thrown to the pavement.

When the accident happened, I'd been looking at a text from Ashley. Normally I glance at a text and get my eyes back on the road. But she texted, *We have something to talk about tonight.* And I was staring at it and trying to get what she meant. Was this good? Was this bad? It was cryptic, to be sure, and I couldn't help but feel like I was in for it, like it wasn't going to be a good night for us.

So I was driving down Mission Boulevard in Jurupa Valley, and when I got on the bridge that leads to Riverside I was staring at that text, and then I felt the car smack into something, and the whole thing lasted a few seconds, maybe just one second, I don't know, it was a flash, just a flash of a moment. My car smacked something hard, and I looked up and hit my brakes, but before the car stopped, before my foot had even reacted and started to push down on the brake pedal, I looked up and saw this guy half on a bike and half in the air, sideways leaning, holding onto a puffed-up trash bag, and he flew off to the right, the trash bag with him, and then the man and bag smacked against the pavement and soda cans flew everywhere and the bike went under my car and there was the sound of metal scraping. And my tires were locked and screeching then when the car had just trampled the bike, and in the moment when the metal bike was being crushed I felt the scraping in my gut, and then when my car finally stopped I hopped out to see what all had happened.

My car was stopped there on the bridge, and I was running around to the other side, and I saw the crushed bike behind my car, and there were cans everywhere, and then I saw Ronnie, the homeless guy, on all fours trying to pick up the cans that fell out of his trash bag.

"Are you okay?" I said to him. "Forget about the cans. Are you okay?" And I knelt down because he was ignoring me and was just all about those loose cans.

And then I patted him on the back, and he said, "Help me, dipshit. Get those goddamn cans over there."

A few good Samaritans stopped and helped us. We gathered his cans up and moved his mangled bike to the side of the road, and I moved my car off to the side to ease up traffic, and someone had called an ambulance and it didn't take long for that thing to come racing in on the scene.

After the blur of the accident had passed, along with the can gathering and all the onlookers moving on, Ronnie sat on the side of the road while a paramedic looked him over, and I was the only one left from the initial crowd after the good Samaritans got back in their cars and moved on. And I fessed up to it. I let everyone know that I was the guy who hit him and that I'd stick around.

One of Ronnie's elbows was all swollen, and his ribs were bruised pretty badly. He had a helmet on—which surprised me, a homeless guy wearing a helmet—but that meant it could have been a lot worse for him. That styrofoam on the inside of the helmet was cracked from the impact.

I let the paramedics take down my info. I gave them all the right numbers, the right address, and so on.

Ronnie said, "Don't worry, man. I'm not going to sue you." He said, "Don't worry, man. I've got insurance."

And I said, "I'd like to pay for whatever bills there are." And I found out what hospital they were taking him to.

But Ronnie said, "My name's Ronnie, man." And that was when I learned his name. And then he said, "I'm a vet, man. I've got insurance, man. Free ambulance rides. Maybe five a year. And when I get there, I'll just go again. I'll just do the minimum, man, and then I'll just go again."

I said, "Let me give you my number."

"I've got a cell phone, man," he said.

"Good," I said. "Let me give you my number, and you call me if I owe you anything."

"You owe me a bike."

"I'll buy you a new bike," I said.

"Really?" he said. "That's nice of you. That's nice of you. But I guess you did hit me first, right?"

"Yeah," I said. "Sure," I said.

The paramedics said they needed to take him to the hospital then. They'd bandaged that swollen elbow, but they said they had to take him in just to make sure there wasn't any internal damage.

Then Ronnie said, "Take my bike and cans down to my camp."

"The wrecked bike?"

"It's good for parts. You owe me. Take it down to my camp. And my cans. Walk down the dirt trail on that side. Walk down for a while till you see that tree over there. See it?"

"Yeah."

"Turn in there and walk down the hill. Then keep walking up more but stay near the side and then you'll see an orange tent. Henry's on a rope, okay. Henry's on a rope so don't get close. He'll fuck you up, man. When you see the tent, just set the bike and cans down. Just set them down and I'll find them later. Don't you go walking to my tent, man. Henry will fuck you up, man."

"I'll just set them down. Henry's your dog?"

"Of course, man. No, he's my wife! What's wrong with you, man? Of course he's my dog."

"Okay," I said, and I was nervous about the damn dog but not even sure yet if I was going to bother walking over there at all.

"And meet me here tomorrow morning. Not here but over there."

He pointed to a fenced-in park at the base of the backside of Mt. Rubidoux.

"That's a dog park. Saturday and Sunday mornings I meet my buddy Ace over there. I'll be there after the sun's up, okay? You pick me up there. Maybe six or seven or eight."

"I'll be there at eight," I said.

The ambulance took off with him, and I picked up his crumpled bike and sack of cans. I followed the dirt path where he'd pointed and got to the tree he was talking about, and then I hesitated.

He's on a rope, I told myself. He's on a rope. So I walked down the slope and entered the dry riverbed. I walked slowly. I crept. I was thief-like in my approach even though I was dropping off someone's stuff and not after anything. In a little bit, I saw the orange tent, and it was still far away and I wasn't getting any closer. It was a dark faded orange. A burnt orange. And around the tent, there were piles of things. Maybe some crates. Maybe some jugs of water. I couldn't tell from the distance. I set the bike and cans down close to the slope's edge like he'd asked. I wasn't about to go walking up to some guard dog at that moment.

And then I just scampered out of there, made it back to my car as quickly as I could, and then realized that it was getting warm and that I was sweating, but luckily I keep an extra deodorant in my glove box, and then I put some on, cranked the AC, and restarted my drive to work.

∾

In my car, I started thinking about the last time I rode a bike, but I couldn't pinpoint it. It had been several years. And then I started thinking about my friend Carlos from elementary school because we would always ride bikes together in the street.

And then I got to thinking about this one time in third grade when Carlos and I wrote and performed a play for his grandma and her friends. We spent hours on the script, hours on the costumes and cardboard backdrops. Then we lugged everything out to his grandma's living room, set it all up. Five old ladies sat on the couch and two wingback chairs. They smacked their lips, drank their tea. One of them pulled a lipstick out of her purse. She puckered and applied. She offered the stick to her neighbor, who took it and applied it, too.

And now you might be thinking, Joe, why is this important? You were just going on about hitting a homeless guy and you haven't even brought in Ashley yet.

So I'll tell you now in case you're wondering. It's all important. All this stuff matters. What I'm telling you is: that lipstick was cherry red. I remember its brightness. Now I might compare the color to an unhappy man's red sports car. I might be tempted to call it Ferrari red, or racing red, since I feel middle-aged, but that stage is still years away since I'm not even thirty, except that we don't know when we're going to die, so maybe I passed my midlife a while back. But it's not Ferrari red because that's a rich man's compensation, and I'm too happy to be unhappy. What I'm saying is: my third grade friend's grandma and her troop passed around a cherry red lipstick. They passed it around like schoolgirls. They passed it around like a joint, but of course, I wasn't thinking that at the time. But now I can imagine them as young women when I couldn't then, their lives brimming with the triumphs and disappointments that brought them to that couch and those wingback chairs, taking comfort in each other and their tea and that cherry lipstick. And you need to know that they applied it carefully, like they were going to the theater, and then they slurped from their cups and waited for the day's entertainment.

This was my first time in a play. I took it very seriously. The play was called *Companion*. We each played an animal you wouldn't expect to be friends with the other. He was a peacock because there were tons of feather boas in the trunk at the foot of his grandma's bed. He stripped down to his undies, and I wrapped the blue boas around his waist, around his chest and arms. Then we took wire hangers and bent them straight, except for the hooks, which we attached to a belt he put on. About twenty metal wires shot out from his back down to the carpet, and I wrapped the green and yellow and turquoise boas up and down those bent hangers. He put on black eyeliner and one of his grandma's blue hats. He looked spectacular. And I don't know where he is now, but I like to think he's here in the world doing spectacular things.

I was a dog. I know, I know. You're thinking, Too boring, Joe. Or, What kind of dog, at least? But neither of us had a dog, so we didn't know breed names, and our thinking was: A) a dog would chase a peacock, so it satisfied the requirement of being a surprising friend, and B) if one animal was wild and extravagant, the second should be mild, reserved.

So I put on his grandma's tan sweatsuit, and we cut out floppy ears from construction paper and taped them to a hat. He wanted to use eyeliner to color my nose black and kind of give me an upward dog smile, but I told him I didn't like other people touching my face, or touching me in general, and he respected that and said, "Ok, just smile the whole time. And maybe pant sometimes when it's not your turn to talk."

And I said, "Sure." And we put on bathrobes to disguise our costumes while we set up the first cardboard backdrop. The first act took place in a school lunchroom. On the cardboard behind us, we'd drawn rows of tables with kids and animals sitting and eating. The living room rug was our stage. We brought out a card table and two folding chairs, then slipped into the hallway and removed our robes. From the wing, we said together, "A play called *Companion* will begin in thirty seconds." His grandma and her friends applauded. Then a hush fell over the living room, and my friend came out in his peacock garb and sat sideways in a chair. This allowed his wire-hanger/feather-boa tail to flow behind him without getting messed up, and it allowed him to face the audience so that he could explain to them that he'd tried to sit at a table with other kids and animals but that they'd all told him to go away. They'd said he was funny-looking and a weirdo and that he smelled bad. Then he explained that it was the first day of school and that he was scared and nervous. I think he talked a bit about where he was from and what brought him to the area. Then he turned his head to face the table, picked up an imaginary sandwich, and chewed the air in an overexaggerated manner. My cue was to come out on the fifth bite. He chewed slowly between each bite, really milking the sadness of the situation. He sighed a lot, too. Then at last I came out and explained that I'd been sitting at a nearby table and that I'd witnessed others being mean to him. I said that I didn't like the table I was sitting at because the animals there were swearing a lot. And then I said, "I told myself to be courageous, so I stood." That's verbatim. You know the way some phrases from your past just stick. I wrote the first part, and he added the last bit. And then we looked at each other like, Wow, we really are a couple of genius playwrights. Though I doubt we knew that word yet.

So then, of course, my doggie-self joined him at the table, and we talked and fake-ate food and agreed to be best friends, and then we got up and announced that it was time to go back to class. The second act doesn't need as much of a recap. We switched out the cardboard backdrops. The new setting was outside of the school, so we'd drawn sidewalks and a road and some cars and the school in the background. Basically, I was walking home and I was distraught because I couldn't find my new peacock best friend anywhere. And I carelessly stepped out into the street, definitely not looking left, then right, then left as we'd been taught, and just when I was about to get run over by a speeding car, my new friend rushed over to me and pulled me back to safety. He clutched me in his arms and explained how he'd just saved me from a reckless driver. His grandma and her friends gasped. His heart knocked against my chest as he held me.

The third act took place in a candy shop. It was the same day. These cardboard backdrops had old-timey countertops and jars of candy everywhere. I don't think either of us had been in a store that was only a candy store, but we'd seen them in movies. We also weren't allowed to walk home after school, but I digress. So after my near-death experience, I said I wanted to buy my new friend a gumball from the candy shop down the street. You know, to thank him for saving me. And he said he wanted to do the same. He said something like, "You know, you saved me, too. Earlier at lunch. You saved me, too."

In the candy shop, my doggie-self picked out a blue gumball for him, and his peacock-self picked out a yellow gumball for me. And these were real props. He had a couple left from his stash, and he wanted to use them for this performance. So we talked for a while in the store, and then we purchased the gumballs with imaginary money, and I popped the yellow one in my mouth, and I bit down on it and chewed. And he popped the blue one in his mouth, but then he gargled and coughed and dropped to his knees, hitting the rug hard, then fell forward onto his chest and shook his legs and arms and then stilled.

I rushed to his side and flipped him over. His grandma flew to the ground and shoved a finger in his mouth and was hooking around. We thought he'd died. But he whispered, "Grandma, Joe, it's fine. This is part of the show." And he rose, and he escorted his grandma back to the couch, and he spit the gumball into his hand, then raised it above his head, pinching it between his thumb and finger to show the audience, and then he looked at me and then back at our audience, and then he gave a monologue as the ghost of the peacock, and I slid to the side, an unknowing viewer now, too, and he talked about the merits of being kind in all moments because you never know which day might be your last, and he talked about how all things are short-lived—joy, pain, pleasure, heartbreak—and those weren't his exact words, but he went on for a while, and then he concluded his speech by standing on the brick fireplace and shouting, "Nothing matters in the world except kindness!"

His grandma and her friends went wild with applause. They stood. They cheered. I think I was even clapping. And then my friend gestured for me to move back to center stage with him, and we held hands and bowed together. Bowing again and again and again and again while the ladies who were once vibrant young women cheered our tenderness and ambition while wearing their cherry lipstick.

Later we rode our BMX bikes until our moms picked us up. While we were riding, I was mad at him, but I never told him. I was thinking, How could you abandon the story we'd planned to tell? I didn't think it was fair that we agreed to have equal parts, but then he ended up shining at the end. But mostly I was upset that the thing I was positive would happen didn't. You know? And you're thinking, Okay, okay. Life lessons. Big deal. People are unpredictable. But you need to know these details: he was popping wheelies on his bike. He was smiling. He was beaming while the air blew through his hair. And I tried to stay on his tail, following his moves, murmuring, "We were supposed to eat gumballs together and be happy."

∾

I parked my car in the lot behind my work, entered through the café's back entrance, and told my boss I was late today because I hit some homeless guy with my car.

And work was work. I lasted my shift and then put in an hour of overtime since we'd gotten new crates of vegetables—red onions, avocados, Batavia lettuce, and so on—and they needed washing, then storing or slicing. My boss wasn't too mad that I'd clocked in an hour late because it was a pretty slow Friday. The place is called Empire Café, which isn't a very good name if you ask me, but the boss chose it because we're all living in what's called the Inland

Empire—Riverside but also San Bernardino, Corona, Jurupa Valley where I
live, and the other southern California cities out here an hour east of Los Angeles, everything that presses up against the mountains, all this land out here
where the summers roast you from May to October, six months of heat almost
always in the nineties at least.

But so that's what he named it, Empire Café, and I mostly make sandwiches there though sometimes I get stuck making drinks too. But I mostly make
sandwiches because I'm really particular about things. I arrange the veggies just
so. I roll up sliced meat like tight cigars. I'm just good at it. So one day when the
boss saw my work he said, "All right, here's our new sandwich guy," and kicked
this guy Larry back onto the espresso machine.

After work, I drove home and got there around 6:00 p.m. The café's in
downtown Riverside, so I drove back over the bridge to get into Jurupa Valley—
I have an apartment out there because the rent is cheaper—and for most of the
day I'd forgotten that I'd hit that homeless guy Ronnie. I mean I didn't forget.
I just wasn't actively thinking about it. But when I had to drive over the bridge
again, of course I thought about it, and my body even reacted to it. Like I shivered recalling the crunch of the bike under my car and was relieved that I didn't
run him over. And I thought about stopping to see if he'd found his wrecked
bike and cans, but then I remembered that I said I'd meet him in the morning
to buy him a new bike, and I had a date with Ashley I needed to shower for, so
I just kept heading home.

At about eight, I met up with Ashley at this restaurant called The Salted
Pig. "Now that's a name," I said, "The Salted Pig. Much better than Empire Café."

"You should start your own café one day," she said. "You could have bookshelves everywhere. A take-a-book-leave-a-book kind of deal. Host literary
events. Have authors read their poems and stories."

Ashley's a professor and a poet. Even though she's so young to have that
job. I mean the professor part. Most poets are young—kids, teenagers, right?
Like all kids are artists. And then in adulthood, in terms of the population, so
very few people are artists or poets in their thirties, forties, et cetera. But I was
saying that Ashley is young to be a professor. Twenty-eight, exactly my age. And
I mean *exactly* my age. How do I know this? On our first date, she was carded,
and I saw her birthday when she held up her license for the waiter to see. And
there it was: 04/23/1988. And maybe I wouldn't have even noticed if it was any
date other than my own. And the waiter didn't card me, and I didn't comment
on us sharing a birthday. I don't know why. Maybe I thought she'd be turned off
by it, like I was encroaching on her space or her life. It was early 2017, and life

16

was brimming, and I imagined how cool it would be to celebrate our twenty-ninth together and then have a whole year under our belts before facing the big thirty together, and so on and so on. But still, I didn't bring the shared birthday thing up. So she's a writer like me, but a real one. I mean, a more accomplished writer than me. At least from what she's said and from what I've read about her online. She hasn't shared her writing with me, and I haven't either. Probably we'll need to do that before she lets me do more than kiss her. They call her an assistant professor, but she doesn't do any assisting. Teaches all the classes on her own. It's just a title for professors when they're still young.

I said, "I like working for someone else right now. I don't really want the stress of figuring out how to go it alone." I wondered what she thought of us as a couple even though we were only three dates in—that night, the day I ran over Ronnie's bike, being our fourth. I wondered if she thought I had enough ambition for someone like her. But she agreed to a second, then a third, then a fourth date, so I told myself not to worry too much about it. We'd first met in the produce aisle of Stater Brothers. I helped her pick out avocados because I was right there getting myself some, and she looked confused, didn't know what shade she needed to be able to make guacamole that day. I said, "This one here is pretty good," and handed her the one I was holding. And then she looked up at me, and I was really taken aback by her eyes. Maybe not so much her eyes, which were a lovely medium brown, but her eye sockets. They were real round and her eyes looked big, and she was just kind of stunning standing there. And her hair was also brown, but darker than her eyes, and it was all wrapped up and held together with a pencil. If she sounds ordinary, I'm doing a bad job describing her. So I found the best avocados for her, felt around longer for hers than I did for my own, and five minutes of chit-chat led to a coffee later that same day. I'd told her I don't do that normally, ask girls out in grocery stores. She'd said, "Good. I hope not."

The waiter brought our drinks over, and Ashley looked around the room, kind of surveying it before she grabbed her wine and took a sip. I'd noticed that she'd done that on the other dates too, kind of took inventory of who was in the restaurant before letting lips meet wine.

This time I asked, "Everything okay?"

She said, "Yeah." She said, "Want to hear a funny story?"

"Always," I said. And I took a sip of my wine. Some red kind, same as Ashley was having. I normally order a beer, but after she ordered her wine and the waiter was staring at me, I just asked for the same thing the lady was having, and I felt like an idiot because I hadn't done that on the other dates, but Ashley smiled, so it was okay.

"Well," she said. "I'm not really supposed to be drinking out in public. In case my students see me. Or some straight-laced professor. Isn't that lame?"

"That's jacked up," I said. "Is that a rule then, about teaching there?"

Ashley taught at Hardin College, which isn't in Riverside but is about twenty minutes south in a tiny town called Coyote Corner. They've got about one thousand students there. The town might be double that. When she got the job at Hardin, she moved to Riverside because it had the most culture, she said, out of the inland cities.

"It's not a rule exactly," she said. "It's not in the contract I signed, but it's implied. Expected even. So here's the story. When I was on my campus visit two years ago, I was interviewing with the provost, and I'd already done my teaching demo, and it had gone really well, and one of the faculty I had breakfast with that morning told me that if candidates do well throughout the day, they get an interview with the president after their interview with the provost, but not everyone gets that far, but because it's a small school and the president wants to have his hand in everything, they only schedule campus visits with candidates when the president is on campus. Am I making sense? Is this making sense? This is boring."

"No," I said. "It makes sense," I said. "It's interesting."

"Ok. Thanks," she said. "If you say so," she said. "So after a long day of this and that, I'm in the provost's office, and he's been asking me questions about my research and writing some but mostly about teaching, and then he starts talking about the history of the school, and he seems proud of their fundamentalist roots, and he's talking about the code of ethics and expectations for students and faculty, and I'm on board with a lot of what he'd said so far except the homophobia, and then he asks me if I drink."

"Can he do that?"

"I mean in this case, I guess so. And I wanted to be honest throughout the whole process. Because I had another year of funding in my program, I didn't have to take a job that year if I didn't want to, but also the job market is terrible right now, so you kind of should take any full-time position you can get your hands on. So he asks me if I drink, and I look at him and I say, 'Well, I do occasionally enjoy a glass of wine with dinner.' And he looks me over. Not in a creepy way. I could tell he was figuring out if he was going to help me at this point. Then he says, 'Well, here's the thing. This is where we're at. The search committee has indicated to me that you are a particularly strong candidate, and I agree with them'—I'm not trying to brag. That's just what he said—"

"Sure," I said. "Of course not."

"So he said I was a strong candidate, and then he said, 'We do have a policy here where we ask our faculty not to drink.' And I said, 'Oh.' And he said, 'Here's the thing. I don't care what you do at your home. I just don't want to hear from some parent or student that you were seen down at Pepito's with a pitcher of margaritas.' And he said, 'I'm going to recommend you for an interview with the president today, and at some point he's going to say to you, We have a policy where our faculty members don't drink. Are you okay with that? And I would suggest to you that the best answer one could give in that situation is, Yes, sir, I am okay with that.'"

"No shit," I said. "Sorry for that, the swearing, I mean, but damn."

"Don't worry about it," she said. "I'm not a nun or something. But isn't that wild? But anyway, yeah, hence my looking over my shoulder before I partake of this heavenly glass of pinot with you at The Salted Pig."

We had a nice dinner, talking about this and that. She asked me about my day at work, but first I told her about hitting the homeless guy Ronnie and how he was okay, or at least I thought so, and how I was going to buy him a new bike in the morning. She said that was nice of me.

When I walked her to her car, we peck-kissed on the lips like we did after date number three, and then she said, "Let's get together tomorrow night if you're free," and that excited me because up until then it had always been me asking.

On the drive home, crossing the bridge again, this time at night with the streetlamps glowing, I realized that I'd forgotten to ask her about the text she'd sent and that she'd never brought it up—*We have something to talk about tonight*—the whole reason I'd rammed into Ronnie in the first place. I texted her right when I got home, asked her about it.

It's nothing to worry about, she wrote. *It was a work-related thing having to do with that conference I went to. A connection leading to a good publication for me.*

Congrats!!! I wrote. *That's wonderful!!!* I wrote. *I feel like a jerk for forgetting to ask.*

You're not a jerk, she wrote. *You're a sweet one*, she wrote. *Good night.*

And I wanted to write so much to her in that moment, because maybe I felt her slipping away, or maybe I just then was realizing how into her I was, but I knew I should let her be and that the only thing to write then was *Good night. Sleep well.* So I wrote that, and that ended our string of texts, and then I stared at my ceiling for a long while, debating going for a night walk or a night drive, debating finding some book to read, but I just stared at the ceiling, considering the patterns in the drywall, the grooves like tiny rivers, dried-up rivers leading to nowhere. I couldn't turn my mind off, so I talked aloud to myself for a while. Because that helps sometimes. Because sometimes I need to hear what I'm thinking to know exactly what I mean. So I said things like, "Perhaps she'll be the one for you. And you'll be the one for her. But maybe not. So try not to act all crazy or do anything crazy. And don't get too obsessed over her like you're doing now. Okay? Try to avoid stuff like this every night. Okay?" And I answered back things like, "You're right. I know." And I said to myself, "I won't. I won't think of her more than I should." But I knew I was just saying that to appease myself. I knew that thoughts can't be controlled like actions.

And while I was talking aloud and studying the ceiling, every now and then I'd pinch a thigh, a forearm, a finger just to make sure I was still whole. It's an odd fear, I guess, one I've mostly outgrown. As a kid, I worried that my mind would disconnect from my body if I stayed up all night thinking instead of sleeping. I'd imagine a ghostly version of myself floating above my body, trying and failing to get back inside. I'd pinch my chest to get grounded again. I'd whisper things to myself like, "Mind, don't you dare leave this body." Now, in bed, Ashley on the mind, I pinched a new piece of skin every ten minutes or so while I talked to myself. I tried to say aloud little stories that I could jot down later. But each one started, "Once there was a boy who loved Ashley," and then it would fizzle out after only a few sentences, a few sentences of hopeful nonsense, things like us living in the woods in a cabin overlooking the ocean where we are famous writers who live obscurely, splashing into the world now and again to greet adoring fans and do cameos in independent films before returning to our clifftop residence. But really, that's not what I want for myself. I'm content to be unknown. I expect that. I can't see a reason why the world would need to know about me when I'm gone. I'm just after a bit of comfort while I'm here.

Maybe tomorrow morning I'll actually meet up with that homeless guy Ronnie and buy him a new bike. Probably Ashley is a fantasy that will fizzle out. Probably Ashley will leave me soon if she even considers us a thing at this point. But somewhere in a burnt-orange tent, Ronnie is thinking of me. Ronnie is thinking of the guy who ran him over, who promised him a new bike in the morning. Ronnie must be curled up with his dog Henry. He must be talking to him, telling him about his crazy day, letting the dog curl into his warmth, saying to him what a good boy he is for killing the rats and never once calling him a failure or a bad owner. Then I said, "Once there was a boy who loved Ashley," and I said, "Once there was a boy destined to be a homeless man in a dried-up riverbed," and I said, "Once there was a dog destined to be a rat killer for a homeless man," and I said, "Once there was a girl who maybe and hopefully was destined to love me but probably isn't and really I'll be okay either way." And I said, "We'll see how this plays out." And I said, "You know how this plays out." And I said, "You're probably right." And I said again and again and again, "Mind, don't you leave this body. Mind, don't you leave this body," until I reached the point when sleep finally took over.

II

The Inspired Painting

ONCE A PERSON LOOKED down from a cloud, and she thought to another person: a landscape with some fountain grass, a tangerine tree, a mild river, a billowy sea, and a snowy mountain is nice for a person to hang on her living-room wall. Because then a person escaping her day for a short moment here with coffee, a short moment here with cup two, and a long moment here with her dead mother's ironing board, can fantasize herself as person skiing, then as dolphin swimming, and then as kitty cat napping in fountain grass while curled up like human child. Later in the day, a person's husband can be staring at the TV with his feet up or sometimes his feet down, and a person can sit beside him while fantasizing herself as person savoring tangerine while tubing downriver, and maybe when a person's husband's long-day lips kiss hers, she tastes sweet juice instead, and maybe when a person's husband rubs a person's inner thigh and suggests, Perhaps on couch, perhaps in bed, a person is on a shiny Christmas sled, zipping and cutting and crying joy, and then shedding her clothes to wash in the hot and salty sea before scouring the canvas for a space to plant something new.

2

I DROVE TO GET Ronnie the next morning. I parked in the lot by the dog park at the base of Mt. Rubidoux. We'd talked on the phone that morning. I'd called just to confirm the time, and he seemed real confused but then remembered that the guy who'd hit him offered to buy him a new bike. Once he figured out who was calling him, he'd said he didn't think I'd show. Said he assumed the number I gave him was a fake. Then he'd said, "Meet me in the dog park." He'd said, "Me and Henry will be in there."

So I went into the dog park, and Ronnie was in there with that dingy dog of his, and he was talking to another old timer who clearly wasn't homeless. The guy's t-shirt and jeans were clean, and he had on an LA Dodgers cap that was pristine—navy blue with white letters. Not a homeless guy's cap because of the whiteness of those letters. And the old timer that wasn't homeless had a dog too, some Dalmatian-looking thing but fatter than the firetruck Dalmatians you see in photos. So not a homeless looking dog.

I walked up to Ronnie and the guy next to him, and Ronnie said, "Ace, this is the guy who hit me. Guy-who-hit-me, this is Ace. I've known him since high school. We meet here on Saturdays and Sundays. He brings coffee and breakfast croissants."

I nodded to Ace, said, "Hi there."

And he shook my hand, said it was nice of me to take Ronnie to get a new bike.

"Sure," I said. "No worries," I said.

We dicked around at the dog park for an hour or so. I was ready to get this over with. But Ronnie and Ace just kept talking. And I could tell Ronnie was crazy. I mean most homeless probably are. Some people like to tell you that there are homeless out there with master's degrees and stuff. People just down on their luck. Doctors even. But let's face it. Most homeless are kind of crazy for one reason or another, and Ronnie was no exception, rambling on about politics, conspiracies, et cetera, et cetera, and he said he was a veteran and a Republican and that he used to work as a roofer and that he went to high school in Riverside with Ace some forty- or fifty-odd years ago. And life happened to both of them, and one of them has a house somewhere nearby and a fat clean dog, and one of them lives in a tent at the river bottom and has a sorry-looking mutt, and yet here they are, old high-school chums, getting their dogs together for weekend playdates while they drink coffee, eat Carl's Jr., and talk nonsense. And I could tell that Ace was just putting up with Ronnie and his crazy talk, kind of humoring him, being polite because of whatever Ronnie used to be, perhaps feeling guilty or maybe just a regular sadness for the change.

So finally we left the dog park, and Ace said it was nice to meet me and that maybe I'd be there tomorrow morning or next Saturday, and I said maybe but I don't have a dog, and he said, "Easy fix."

But anyway Ronnie and I left, and I started walking to where my car was in the parking lot, but he didn't follow, and when I looked at him Ronnie said, "Remember Henry?"

And I nodded an oh-yeah.

And he said, "This way. We'll drop him off, then get that bike."

And I thought about saying that I'd just wait there, but I didn't want to be rude, but even more so I think I wanted to go check out that tent space again even though I admit it's kind of freaky down there in the river bottom.

So I followed him down a paved path and then off on an unpaved path and down the slope into what was once a wide river but is now a dried-up river bottom with a sad stream way down on the other side. It's still called the Santa Ana River. But it's just a trickle of water, a slow, usually dirty stream, at least where Riverside and Jurupa Valley meet. Maybe the Santa Ana is bigger somewhere else. I'm not sure where it flows from. Maybe it's a real river somewhere else.

We walked on the side without the stream, and there were weeds and shrubs and wildflowers everywhere because it was March and we'd had a really rainy winter by Inland Empire standards. We walked under the bridge I'd hit him on yesterday morning, and there was the regular graffiti everywhere and strewn beer bottles and old abandoned blankets, but it still looked scenic on account of the rare green everywhere. Soon enough all that green would turn to brown and stay brown for at least half a year. Except for the trees and shrubs growing by the stream. They'd stay green, and then in the long terrible summers you can tell where there's still some water left because of the meandering green line.

So we walked under the bridge. And it's a long bridge, a long bridge help-ing cars get over more dirt and weeds than water. And we came out on the side I'd been on yesterday. And eventually, the terrain looked familiar and I saw his burnt-orange tent up ahead. The whole time we walked, Henry stayed right by his side, no need for a leash, and Ronnie stayed quiet, which was fine by me.

At his campsite, he tied Henry to a tree, and the dog plopped down in the shade.

"He sleeps in the tent with me at night," Ronnie said, "but in the day I keep him out here to guard my stuff. He's old now, but he'll bite your balls off, man, if you mess with him. Ha! Bite your balls off, man."

"I believe it," I said.

"And you gotta keep your tent zipped up," he said. "Rodents and things. And oh man, Henry's still good at catching rats. Chews the bastards up. That's why his rope is long, you know. He still needs to be mobile out here."

"You've got it all worked out," I said.

"Let's see about that bike," he said.

In my car Ronnie ran his hands along the dash. "Smooth," he said. "Ace's car has a smooth dash like this too."

"That's good," I said.

"Yeah," he said. "I was in his car a few weeks back, a few months back, and it was in one of those rainstorms, and because there was a chopper flying around over tent city—you know, tent city, more like tent town—"

I nodded.

"Because there was a chopper flying around saying, be advised, man, get out of the river bottom, you hear, flash flood and all that, be advised and all that, and it kept circling and circling, kept saying be advised, flash flood, be advised, remove yourselves from the river bottom. So I'd been sticking out the rains no prob, but, man, a chopper flying overhead. I thought there must be some serious shit on the way. They must've seen some big old pile of water way up on the other side making its way. But I'm pretty lucky because my spot is high up down there. Did you see?"

I nodded.

"Yeah, so you know. My stuff's kind of high up to the side and it's much lower on the other side. So I zipped the tent, took what I needed, took a bag with my best stuff, my radio and my science fiction reads, and I scrambled up the side with my bag and my bike and left the rest, and of course, Henry was by me, and I just took that warning for some reason, because, let me tell you, that chopper guy's voice was warning me like the voice of God. Be advised.

Flash flood. That's biblical. Did you know that? Flooding. So I took the warning because it was a chopper. Anything else, like some guy on foot, I'd say fuck you. But a chopper. I listened. And so then I called up Ace, and Ace picked us up. And I'm fortunate to have him because most people like me only have other people like me. But Ace wouldn't take me to his house. And I knew that was the drill because he'd done that to me before, asshole. You know he's my buddy when I say that. But the fucking asshole won't let me sleep at his house in these situations. But he's a good buddy because he takes Henry for me, Ace does. He lets Henry stay at his house, and he drops me off at the shelter. And the other time he had to do that. Not the chopper time with the flood. The other time was when they were clearing out bushes and things and maybe doing a census or something. No, wait. No, they were just clearing out debris but told people to pack up. I said fuck off but still packed my tent, and Ace kept it and Henry and took me to the shelter, and then two days later I'm back out there putting my tent up after the circus left town."

I didn't know what to say after all that, but we were almost at the K-Mart on Arlington, so I just said, "It sounds like Ace is an okay guy."

And he said, "Fuck you, man. Ace is the best."

And I said, "It looks like we're here."

And he said, "You know I'm just messing with you, man. You know I'm just messing with you."

And I said, "Sure. No worries, man." And we hopped out of my car and went inside the K-Mart.

The bikes were lined up in the back of the store, past the camping gear, and Ronnie eyed some pop-up chairs before seeing the bikes and rushing over like a little kid. Picture this old guy in his sixties, jeans dirty, layers of shirts—no sweatshirt—just like four t-shirts on, all brown or tan. Picture this guy with a long gray beard and frizzly hair, thick sturdy nose, sagging cheeks a little, more wrinkle lines than he probably should have, real tan tough skin, leathery. So picture him rushing over to the wall of bikes like a ten-year-old, sliding his hands along the cool metal frames, testing out the seats, sitting upright while getting a feel for the handlebars, going from bike to bike, testing this and that, looking, considering.

"Does it matter which one?" he said. "Are any off limits?"

I said, "Choose whichever. Take your time." And I remembered what that feeling was like. I remembered being a kid and having my dad or mom with me when I was allowed to pick out something—a bike, a video game, some item I couldn't afford yet on my own and needed their help with. And I remembered the weight of the decision and the consideration involved. And here was this old homeless guy Ronnie, smiling like a little kid while he was sitting on a new bike, one foot on either side of the frame, sitting proud like he was a biker at a stoplight or something.

I hadn't considered how we'd take the bike back, and Ronnie offered to ride it home, but his elbow was still bandaged, and I owed him at least a ride back to his tent with his new bike since I'd rammed into him and didn't even have to pay any medical bills. So I left Ronnie and his bike standing outside of my locked car while I went back inside and bought some rope and a tarp to protect my roof, and I also grabbed that pop-up chair he'd been wide-eyed about and a case of Gatorade stacked at the end of a row.

When we got back to the bridge, I parked in a dirt lot closer to where his setup was instead of over at the paved lot by the dog park. We walked along a dirt trail above the river bottom, and then we came to the right opening, and he guided his new bike down the slope, and I carried the case of Gatorade with the chair folded on top. Damn case was heavy.

Henry was sitting up staring at us, and Ronnie put up the kickstand on his new bike and then unclasped the rope. Henry sniffed the bike and then walked a circle around the tent and then plopped down in a new shade spot. Ronnie surveyed the area, looking over at some tents off in the distance.

"They're getting closer," he said. "It used to be only me over here. Now they're creeping in. Too many people out here. I'll probably move on soon. No, fuck that. This is my spot."

"Ronnie," I said, "Ronnie, I've got to get going now. You set up now? Anything else I can do?"

"Thanks for the bike," he said. And then he said, "Lesbians. In those tents. Lesbians. I hear them at night. Loud noises. Groanings. I think they're lesbians. Kind of grunting and groaning all night. Hard to read. I read at night but can't waste the batteries. I'll need to ride to the library today or maybe walk. I'll need to plug my phone in somewhere. Thanks for the bike, man," he said again. "It's a good one. It's a motherfucker of a bike, this one. Hot damn, it's a sweet one."

"All right," I said. "No worries," I said. And then I meandered down the dry riverbed until I came across the opening near my car.

∾

I went home and showered. It was late morning, but it felt like it should be later in the day. I put on fresh clothes and started the wash. I didn't know what to do. I called up Ashley and picked up lunch to bring over. We'd had plans to meet for dinner, but I was hoping she'd spend the day with me, and she did. I brought over tacos. We ate, and chatted, and watched a movie—*Casablanca*—her idea, which was good because it meant that maybe she was falling for me. We stayed in for dinner, too, ordered pizza.

When it was late, she asked me if I wanted to stay over, pointing to the couch while she said it. I said, "Yeah, of course." She got ready for bed and came out of the bathroom wearing these enormous PJs, these baggy striped deals, white and blue stripes. She looked hot, adorable too, but she looked real good in those PJs. I brushed my teeth with my finger. We kissed for a while. She had a studio apartment, real spacious though, kind of like a loft I guess, so everything was in one large room: her bed and dresser, her desk and many bookshelves, the couch and TV, all of it spread around the room in their own little stations. She had prints of paintings everywhere. Not cheap posters in frames, but like nice-looking prints. Some were even textured. I recognized a few Kahlo self-portraits, a crazy Bosch I liked, and a Dali I'd never seen but could tell was him. And I was glad the Dali wasn't *The Persistence of Memory*, the one with those melting pocket watches in the sparse landscape. It's a good painting and all, but when I was in college and I'd visit a girl's dorm room, I think they all had that poster on the wall, probably because they sold it in the campus bookstore. And hanging out with one of them once and a few other people, some guy from a philosophy class we were all in tried to get real deep in discussion over that poster of Dali, talking about what's real and what's not real and how can we distinguish dreaming from reality, and I wanted to smack him in the face and say, That's how, but I've never been very outgoing and so I nodded and tried to get a word in now and then. I don't know where any of those people are now or what they're doing with their lives.

In those baggy PJs, Ashley crawled into her bed, and she kissed me again, and then she turned off her bedside lamp and said, "Good night."

And I respected that and said, "Good night." And then I shuffled over to her couch, kicked off my shoes, and pulled the throw blanket over me, staring at her ceiling, comparing it to the one in my apartment, and then wondering why it was that in recent years I'd spent so much of my time by myself instead of seeking out others. And I wondered how Ashley had sized me up. Some guy who was roughly her age—as far as she was concerned (Do people ever *hope* to meet and date someone with the exact same birthday? Just curious.)—some guy who studied English like her, while scraping by (unlike her) and dropping his philosophy second major and taking six years to complete his degree partially due to his easygoing outlook on things and partly due to his mom dying and his closest childhood friend taking his life within a year of each other. And I was thinking, What does she think of me working in a café and making enough for rent and groceries and not really having ambition apart from that as far as I could see? Unless something came along, of course. But I wasn't really seeking anything out, because, well, what did I really want besides her who(m) I just met? The *m* was on account of my mentioning Mom, who perhaps had no greater joy in life than correcting people's grammar. Commenting on their figures behind their back being a close second.

Lying there, I was thinking, How much of my life will I tell Ashley? How much about my dwindling friends and family members? How many of my stories will she want to hear? And I was thinking, Should I tell her that I once spent half a year pretending to be deaf so I wouldn't have to talk to people? Except at work, and even there I was monk-quiet unless I was forced to talk. Maybe so. It's a story. And the whole experiment worked well until a trio of high school boys from the California School for the Deaf saw me signing in Target, and saw me with my pad of paper communicating with the check-out person, and they glimpsed me out as a fake, and they threatened me in the parking lot, and I signed, Fuck off, because I wasn't going to treat them any different than I would anyone else. And they signed, Eat shit, Hearing Boy. We'd kick your ass if there weren't so many people around. And they had lightning quick hands and facial expressions, and I could translate their meaning, but my own signing was slow and clumsy. I signed, then gestured, Follow me. And we walked behind the Target where there's an empty dirt lot at the base of a hill. On the other side of the hill, there's a cemetery with green, green grass, but this side was dirt and boulders with graffiti. I turned around, and the boys stopped, and I signed a rough version of, I don't like talking to people. I've been watching signing videos on YouTube. I'm acting deaf for me, not to insult you. One boy signed, You need to stop that. Another boy picked up a stick and signed, Or we will kick your ass. I signed, You can come hit my face with your fist but not the stick. I signed, I will not move. The third boy signed, Buy us some beer, and don't let us see you mocking us again. I signed, Okay. I brought them back a twelve pack of 805 in cans. I signed, I do admire you. Two of them signed, Thanks. The one who'd had the stick signed, Get the fuck out of here.

I started talking again more regularly after I'd been called out, or signed out, and it was a couple months after that when I'd run into Ashley in the grocery store. And now there I was on her couch, restless. She started to snore like a bunny. Or I mean the little snores I was hearing sounded so cute I imagined that if a bunny were to snore it would sound like her. Because who knows what a bunny snores like? I wanted to get off the couch and nuzzle up beside her. Even if she wasn't ready for sex, I just wanted to watch her sleep and breathe her in, maybe fool around a bit under the covers since all we did was kiss, or maybe even just rub up against each other with our clothes on, like we were teenagers and not actually adults with only two-thirds of our lives remaining if we were fortunate. But I just stayed on the couch and ached. If I were in a medieval romance, my body would be all distorted from this love-longing. All swollen up or emaciated. Probably the latter. Cheekbones protruding unhealthily, ribs popping out, for how could I eat victuals when she denies me her *bele chose*—until, until, until (read/listen further), she comes to me on my death bed and joins me in my death bed and now we've replaced death with a word that means life but is more suggestive and less familiar (whatever that word is), and since she has saved me I would leap onto the back of her bicycle as she pedals by in the fresh morning, and I would kick my feet out and say, Wee, Wee, Wee, while she directs us to wherever she was going.

Eventually, I fell asleep but then after a few hours, I got up to pee. On my way back to the couch I stopped near her bed. She slept on her stomach and her left leg dangled off the mattress. Her PJs rode up to her knee, so her calf was exposed, smooth and shiny even in the dim light. Her foot was snug in its yellow sock. I crouched beside her bed and licked her leg, a long slow lick, then darted for the couch and buried my face in a cushion while I moaned, savoring the mix of salt and jasmine lotion in my mouth.

3

IN THE MORNING I WOKE to unfamiliar brightness, needing to take a minute to get my bearings and remember where I was. Then I tasted her lotion in my mouth, and I licked my lips to taste the salt of her skin, too, but sadly the flavor was gone.

Her couch was comfortable, and I slept soundly. The studio was opened up. It was on the second floor, and Ashley had pulled back the curtains and opened some of the windows. She'd made her bed, and there was no trace of her. In the kitchenette, there was a pot of coffee and an empty mug with a note under it. She'd gone to church, told me to make myself at home, said she thought about waking me to invite me but wanted to let me sleep. I couldn't believe the time. It was 10:00 a.m. The last thing she said on the note was that she picked out this mug for me. It was a Christmas mug, a big Rudolph face, big red nose and antlers. Was this a good sign? I wondered. What other mugs were in her cabinet? Well, there was an Oberlin College mug, a Chicago Symphony Orchestra mug, a World's Best Daughter mug, and a pair of floral patterned teacups with saucers. Which one would she choose for a future lover? One might think one of the two matching teacups, but they were small and didn't look practical to drink out of, so I supposed Rudolph was as decent a sign as I could hope for.

I filled the mug and sipped it while walking around her place. I went to the bookshelves first, set the coffee on her desk while thumbing through the books' spines. There were some novels in there I'd heard of. She had some philosophers even, like Augustine and Aquinas. Maybe theologians is more like it, I suppose. And she had C. S. Lewis, more than just Narnia, which seemed obligatory for young, intellectual Protestants. The few I knew in my philosophy classes quoted Lewis heavily in all their papers. Then there were three bookshelves devoted only to poetry. So many slim books. Who knew so many books of poetry were out there? I suppose I should have, but the truth is I mostly read poetry in the big anthologies that were assigned in my classes. I jotted down some names on a sheet of paper. I recognized some of them from one of our early dates. "Who do you read?" I'd asked. And she rattled off names and names and names. I must've looked confused because then she said, "They're like the Ernest Hemingways of women poets." And then she said, "Forget that. I can't believe I said that, the Ernest Hemingways of women poets. No, forget that. They're just poets. They're great poets." Standing alone in front of her bookshelf, I jotted down a title from Glück and one from Nezhukumatathil, jotted down another from Sharon Olds and one from Tracy K. Smith with a Pulitzer sticker on it. I thought I'd start with those four, order them online, study up on them, and impress Ashley with conversation later.

I slid the books back in and sat at her desk. Sipped on the coffee some more. Opened up her drawers. Flipped through some papers. Found a large envelope buried under some scratch papers with some in-process poems scribbled on them. On one page the phrase *Wind scratching his name on the window* was circled, and the phrase *Wind yelling through the respirator* was crossed out. There were more lines crossed out than circled. The lines were definitely just fragments, not like done poems at all. On our second date, I fessed up and said that I wrote a bit too. "Not real writing like you do," I'd told her, "just jottings I keep in a book, only handwritten so far." She wanted to know if they were poems or stories. That seemed important to her, and I didn't want to infringe on her territory. I said I'd always thought of them as poems even though they're usually each a long paragraph, but maybe they weren't really poems. I said there's always a little story. Always something happens. Little stories in poems. I like beginning with the word *Once*. I know that's been done a lot, I said. I know about modern fairy tales and all. But I still like it. I write down *Once* and then see what happens. She'd said, "They sound like fictions, not poems." And I said she's probably right because she probably is. She offered to look them over for me. She offered to help me edit them, sharpen them. I said thanks. I said maybe one day, maybe one day farther down the road. She said, "Maybe some of those paragraph stories will break free, and you'll have a proper short story. Maybe one of them wants to be a novel." I said, "We'll see." I said, "One paragraph is usually all I can handle."

The envelope from her desk had photos in it too. I put her poem drafts back and looked through the photos. She came from a good-looking family. Had lots of friends around her too. Lots of shots in the snow. Lots of shots from college and what looked like grad school gatherings. She probably missed her friends. Probably the cold too. Probably couldn't stand the long summers out here. There were some pictures of her with the family dog, some kind of gray and white dog with pointy ears. I didn't know what kind that was called. I was looking for pictures of her with an old boyfriend but didn't find any. A good sign, I knew.

I wanted to stay there and go through more of her things, but I wasn't sure exactly how much time I'd have. I didn't know when her service started and how long it ran for. Maybe I'd have another half hour or so. Maybe she'd be back any second. I felt like I shouldn't be there when she got back. I liked her and wanted to make sure she liked me. I felt like I needed to be gone when she got back, like that would help my chances somehow, didn't want to seem too clingy or like I didn't have anywhere else to be off to. I got up from her desk and went over to her dresser just for a minute. I took a few more sips of coffee and then set the mug on the dresser and slowly opened her drawers. Her shirts and jeans and sweaters—sweaters she didn't need here in the desert—were all folded perfectly. Her underwear was perfect too. Not too racy, not too plain. Just the right amount of suggestion. No thongs but some had lace. The cotton ones were dual colors. A solid yellow with blue fringe, or striped ones of orange and blue, purple and green. Not much pink though. Most of the undies had Old Navy labels, and they definitely looked like the type of undies a store like that would sell even though I'd never stepped foot in one. All that brightness and just the shape of her undies made me want to be on a cruise with her sipping daiquiris. Those undies just screamed *Strawberries! Rum! Ice! Blender!* I became aware of my own dullness: jeans and a plain black or plain white shirt practically every day. In my head I was all, You should wear the purple and green undies like a hat and do jumping jacks, just for shits and giggles, you know. But I knew that was dumb, and I said to myself, "That's dumb." I closed her underwear drawer and was pleased with myself for not being weird, and then I stared at her bundles of socks, little boulders folded into each other, all of them paired up perfectly, no unmatched strays. And they were bright too, but there were also dull colors mixed in. I pulled out a lavender pair with tiny white snowflakes and spread them out on top of the dresser. They were long like soccer socks. And too thick for out here. And then a car door slammed outside, and I startled and pushed the drawer in, and my mug shook and some coffee spilled on the socks and the dresser.

At the window, I saw that it wasn't her outside. All the same, I thought I should go. I put the damp socks in my pocket and wiped up the spilled coffee. Then I downed the now lukewarm liquid left in the mug and washed it and put it back in her cupboard. I put my shoes on and wrote her a note, but wasn't sure what to say exactly, so I wrote, *Thanks for the coffee! Delicious. Hope you had a nice service. Talk soon. Joe.*

Ashley attended the old Methodist church on Brockton, said there was a good mix of oldies and young folks there. She said a church needs gray hairs and that too many of the new churches just have young people. She loves talking to elderly women, she said once. Her friends Krystal and Janice go there, too, a real-deal couple sitting together right there in one of the front pews with their boy between them, and everyone's welcoming and accepting. I said it sounded like a nice place. We'd run into Krystal and Janice on our second date. They'd been together for years and knew Riverside better than I did. They chatted with us for a few minutes until they got their table. They told us that next time we needed to check out The Salted Pig. They were good people. I was a little surprised when Ashley'd introduced them as friends from church. I thought that was a good thing, and I didn't want to seem shocked by it, so I stayed quiet and nodded like it was no big deal. When Ashley told me over dinner that they had a boy, biological with sperm donor, I said right away how great that was but then had to think it over privately to tease out what I really thought. And I thought this: you know what, at least he won't know what it's like to have a dad be there and then leave; you know what, at least there is only a very small chance one mom leaves the other mom for a more vibrant gal with thick dark hair and enormous hoop earrings.

On my way home from Ashley's place, I thought about taking Brockton and driving slow to see if the service was done and maybe see if people were hanging around chatting, maybe join them, but I just went the quick way back to my neck of the woods, just went the regular route. When I crossed the bridge from Riverside to Jurupa, I looked over into the dog park to see if Ronnie and Ace were there. But it was too late for them. They would have been there early. Now there was a crowd of latecomers, and I knew they weren't down there anymore.

III

Once a Boy Woke Up
in Sweat or Piss

ONCE A BOY WOKE UP in sweat or piss. He tossed his sheets and mattress pad and jammies and his body into a steaming bath. He soaped these things. He got out and hang-dried the fabrics and towel-dried the body, then tiptoed in his robe to the laundry room adjacent to his sleeping mother. He fingered the collection of spray scents, stopping this time on a maroon canister in the red section. He hoped for cranberry but couldn't be sure in the gray light. Plus the shelf was high and he didn't want to disturb his sleeping mother, so after his palm gripped the cool metal, he slipped down the hallway into the comforts of his room. Door closed. Knob locked even though it's the kind that can be opened from outside with a quarter or a butter knife. Light on. The great reveal. Drum roll. He lifted the spray can above his head like a trophy and saw *Spiced Apple*, and he thought, Intriguing, I wouldn't have picked you but I'm happy you're here. And the boy sprayed, sprayed, sprayed the mattress that he sometimes sweats on and sometimes pees on, and he returned the glorious canister to its collection like a ninja or a mime, then darted to his bathroom to check on his sheets and jammies. They squirmed, dangling above a raging AC vent. He knew he'd rise before his mother, make his bed and slide into his jammies, and he'd unlock his door, and he'd pretend to wake up for the first time with his mother standing above him saying, "That's my good man, my dry little man," but for now he approached his bed again, and he shed his robe and lay naked in the spiced apple drying on his mattress and his skin, filling his nose, supplying his brain with images of autumn in a place where the weather cools and the kids go on hay rides beneath yellowing leaves, shouting, "Wee, Wee, Wee."

4

I SHOWED UP AT Hardin College on the Wednesday after I stole Ashley's socks. I didn't mean to keep them. I was planning on washing them and slipping them back in her drawer, but the coffee turned the snowflakes to mud and I just had to hope she thought she'd misplaced them. Hardin is one of those small private colleges that likes to think it's exclusive, but all you need to get in is a pulse. And then a checkbook. Actually just a pulse and a loan application.

I'd never been there before, and now that Ashley and I had been dating for almost two months, I thought it was time to check it out. I asked her a few weeks back if I could meet her for lunch one day, but she said she's usually too busy and just eats during her office hours. I couldn't tell if she didn't want me there or if she really was too busy. Maybe she didn't want to mix her work life with her personal life. Me? I think you have to be able to mix the two. I think for a relationship to be successful one partner needs to be able to pop into another's work place and be received with excitement or tenderness or even just acceptance—certainly not annoyance, certainly not frustration. My plan for today was just to walk around and get a look at the place. I had her teaching schedule and office hours written on a scrap of paper in my pocket, but I wasn't yet sure if I would run into her or just tour the place without her knowing I was there. I wanted to see her, of course. I always want to see her. But I didn't know if it would be a smart move or not to surprise her at this stage in our courtship.

I parked off campus because I didn't have a parking decal and I didn't want to pay for a visitor pass. Then I put on a backpack and strolled through the front entrance. The backpack was just for show. I figured I should look like a college student while I was lurking about. So the thing wasn't sagging empty on my back, I threw in those poetry books I'd ordered and Ashley's long, thick socks. It was late morning and Ashley was teaching a poetry writing class. I didn't know where it was, but I knew I couldn't sit in on it since it had only a few students in it. So I just walked around the little campus.

There was grass everywhere even though this was technically the desert and all the inland cities were in a drought. The water bill must have been thousands of dollars each month, and I suppose the administration thought it was necessary since they'd probably have a hard time selling the kids and their parents on the idea of attending a grassless college. Cactuses—cacti—everywhere instead of those lovely flowers by the front entrance and in the tree planters everywhere. Maybe geraniums are what those are? I'm not sure. But they're lovely, as was this day, as were those sweet students everywhere. I'm not old. I know that. Even though I've heard other late-twenty-somethings talk like they're old and wise. I'm neither. Mid-level intelligence, to be sure. But I did feel old walking around that campus. I meandered. I eavesdropped. I sat under a tree in the shade and overheard the most fascinating things. I pulled out my copy of *Life on Mars*, fresh from my mailbox. The title seemed appropriate for the Inland Empire. I don't go to Los Angeles often. The freeways are disasters now. Traffic from 6:00 a.m. to 8:00 p.m. Lanes closed for construction in the late night and early morning. But L.A. is okay here and there once you're inside the city. Or its many cities. Once you're planted on a barstool it's okay. But anyway, there are times I've driven out from L.A. to Jurupa Valley in the daytime, and I'm traveling along the foothills, and the mountain range turns from semi-green to brown and dead. There's green bushes dotting the L.A. county range, especially after spring, and then you get to Jurupa and it looks like Mars. We've got these hills and mountains that are rock and dirt and different shades of brown and red and tan, and I don't notice what it's like until I get that perspective. That point of comparison. And I remember once thinking when I drove out of semi-green L.A. and then got to my apartment complex and really focused on the rocky dirt hill behind me—I remember really thinking, This place is like Mars. And now there I was at a table and chairs on the campus of Hardin, a mirage in Mars, a dot of grass and flowers and trees that would all die if left to the elements, all die if it weren't for the thousands of gallons of water tossed on them day after day after day. So I felt like I was in a diorama in the middle of Mars. I pictured the administrators of Hardin like gods above a little box, laying grass down here, moving buildings around, sprinkling soil around the buildings and jamming in flowers and trees with their thumbs, pushing them real good to make sure the roots smushed down and took hold.

Then I sat in a metal patio chair in this quaint area set up for students to read or socialize or eat or whatever, and I sat alone but others clustered at nearby tables, and I cracked *Life on Mars* and dove in. I read while I listened. But that's not real reading, is it? I listened while I half read. I prioritized listening. I wanted to absorb everything around me, and I knew I could reread the poems if I was too distracted. The tree I was under canopied me and the students closest to me. They were talking about double predestination. They were so serious, this guy and four gals, and he spoke like a woman. Or maybe the women spoke like men. Or what I mean is, you couldn't tell there was a guy in the group and four women. What I mean is, he didn't dominate the conversation. What I mean is, they did dominate just as much. It was five people talking. It was five people talking about things they can't quite understand because of the curious mixture of their age, ability, and topic, but, you know, the first thing that struck me was: hey—this is nice for these kids, who, in this moment, were equally feminine and masculine in how they gestured and spoke, but their head space was different, of course, because he must have been in love with at least one of them and must have fantasized about at least one of them but was also imagining if he could be happy with any one of them, but also as a product of his sheltered Protestant megachurch pastel-shaded upbringing, he was probably wondering if one of these bright young girls was his soulmate. I've never been married. And I've had only a couple serious girlfriends. Insignificant dates here and there, but only two serious girlfriends, maybe three. I'm no expert. But what I know is that there are thousands of people in the world any one of us could be happy with, have a good life with, and that should terrify us and comfort us. And the sooner these ambitious young folk realize that, the sooner they can abandon the myth of the soulmate, wondering if she or he is right there in front of them as they philosophize jargon, and instead they can try a person or two on for a while and see if this would do or not do for a stretch of years, waiting until someone fits pretty good and provides more moments of joy than stress or sadness. I think this now. I was thinking it then. But in my organs Ashley, Ashley, Ashley was stirring—in my head, in my chest, my stomach, my groin, even my skin, and I was a hypocrite because I wanted only her and if she would not have me I had decided in some small space in my head that I would become in my apartment a desert hermit who battles demons and maybe writes a thing or two worthy to be read by a few people who could benefit from a recounting of torment and faith and small true things.

What was my reading and listening experience like—balancing *Life on Mars* with the conversation of young folk who want to know the unknowable, who have tight skin and too much innocence? I can't do it justice. I can't write down the overlap. I can't explain it. But it was a pastiche of wonderful naiveté and optimism, and sexual energy and piousness, pure piousness, it seemed, and curiosity, lots of curiosity. And of course there was Tracy K. Smith, whose first poem title licked my eyes in all caps—THE WEATHER IN SPACE—and I thought about the title. Does space have weather? I guess it does. It must. But I always think of it as being the same, unchanging. And I glanced up from the off-white page, and I took in the fivesome, and they were just so lovely: pristine shoes, delicate hands all around, enough diversity in skin tones to make the cover of a college brochure. He had Michigan vowels that marked him as not being from southern California, and he probably had Dutch or German or Scandinavian ancestors, like me on my mom's side, but I've also got a lot of Portuguese, which is why people always say I'm so tan when it's just my complexion, and my hair is walnut brown for most of the year when I get sun, and a little darker from December to February, but not much. And it's why Mom always said I couldn't sit still and had a strong impulse to roam, roam, roam. And I know she said that to knock my dad's blood in me, since he obviously hurt her, but I take it as a compliment since having energy and being an explorer I consider positive traits. So he sounded like he was from the upper Midwest, and Ashley is a Midwest girl who sounds like she's from a newsroom from the Nineties, meaning she didn't have any sounds or turns of phrase that marked her as being from somewhere in particular, but now luckily it seems like maybe the mass media is getting on board with accepting different speeches and realizing that everyone has an accent, et cetera, et cetera. And the four other students also sounded like they had a Californian or western dialect, like me, which again, aside from differences in vocab sounds to me like so much of the middle part of the middle country, like Ashley, a bit down on the map from that guy's speech with his long o's. But I'm digressing and really only have limited knowledge of all of this from being an inquisitive undergrad in years past.

And what did the other four students look like? I remember the guy because he was the only guy, and really I remember his voice more than his appearance, and now as I reflect, as I'm putting this story down, the four female students look like Ashleys even though at the time I do remember thinking, What a diverse group, which is why I said that above, but Ashley strikes out other faces—she's a glint on a window—so maybe two of the girls had skin darker than Ashley's and maybe two of the girls had skin lighter than Ashley's, and maybe their hair was curly or straight or frizzy or wavy or long or short. I don't know. Their tones blend to Ashley. And their features blend to Ashley. A nose slightly leaning to the left. Slightly, mind you, shouting, Exact symmetry is boring town. Hair thick, a deep brown. Flowing down her back when she lets it. Sometimes it's pushed to the side and falls down a shoulder and onto her chest. Sometimes she corrals the strands super quick and wraps them in a bun-type thing on the back of her head. I like when I see her with her hair wrapped up behind her like that and then get to watch her release it, get to watch it unravel down past her neck and fan her shoulders and back. It's hair that begs to be sniffed by the right person. I wondered then if Ashley taught her classes with her hair up or down, and I looked forward to maybe catching a glimpse of her on campus.

But I remember their conversation. No doubt it will be impossible to capture the pure blend of the sweet fivesome's noises—whether words or sighs—gliding through my ear canals and the text of Smith's lines—its format, the letters inked into paper—and how they met in my head, what I was seeing and hearing. I'll fail to capture it. But here's an effort at a script to the scene:

> Smith: *Is God being or pure force? The wind / Or what commands it? When our lives slow . . . /* (Kid 1: If God predestines some for salvation, doesn't that mean he actively made others to be left out of heaven? Isn't all predestination double predestination? Am I missing something?) Smith: *When our lives slow / And we can hold all that we love, it sprawls / In our laps like a gangly doll. When the storm . . . /* (Kids 2 and 3: You are missing something. Yes, you are. It's not like that. It's not an active condemnation. It's just like a subtle thing. No, that's not what I mean. Yes, you're on the right track. It's like, the people who are not predestined to be with God in heaven were not created for the purpose of being damned. That's not why they were created. They just didn't get chosen, I guess.) Smith again, because I remember I read this sentence three or four times: *When our lives slow / And we can hold all that we love, it sprawls / In our laps like a gangly doll.* [Me: Wow, in our laps like a gangly doll, wow, in our laps like a gangly doll.] Smith again: *When our lives slow / And we can hold all that we love, it sprawls / In our laps like a gangly doll. When the storm / Kicks up and nothing is ours, we go chasing . . . /* (Kids 4 and 5: I don't like that. I can't get on board with that. Me too. I agree. I think anyone can be saved. I can't think otherwise. I'll never think otherwise.) Smith: *we go chasing / After all we're certain to lose, so alive— / Faces radiant with panic.* [Me: Yes, amazing. Faces radiant with panic . . . all we're certain to lose . . . we go chasing / After all . . . Faces radiant with panic . . . radiant with panic.] Smith, implied to me: Read it again and again, carry it with you on your tongue, taste *gangly doll* and *radiant with panic* as needed throughout the day, reread to reorient this weird place we're currently residing in, to have yet another angle to make you less an asshole and more a person, because a person breathes, a person breathes and is kind when there is no reason not to be kind; the problem comes with being threatened; the problem comes with thinking that this is it and

this is it and this is all there ever was and can ever be. (Kids 1, 2, and 3: I'm not sure; I'm just not sure.) (Kid 5: Good. Because I am. I know what I believe. Anyone can receive grace. I'd kill myself if I knew there was a God who deemed that some could not be saved.) (Kids 1, 2 and 4: Don't say that. Yes, don't say that.) (Kid 5: Don't worry, you guys. I'm not at risk. It was just a way to get my point across.) [Me: Kids 1, 2, and 4 are recast as Greek Chorus, shouting, Oh no! Oh no! Don't be at risk, sweet sibling in Christ. Anything but that! Don't be at risk!—singing, singing—Don't be at risk! Don't be at risk!] [Me: Kid 5 is recast as Enlightened Person 1; I want to smell her hair and lick that hairless forearm with the small tattoo of a dove with olive branch in beak, but too many unlikely things would have to fall in place to make that happen.]

I stood then. I closed my book and reread the rest of the volume later at home. I grabbed a coffee at a café connected to the tiny campus library. And then I walked around some more. Sipped my coffee and overheard more conversations. Studied all these sweet students. Made my way to Baines Hall, where I knew Ashley's office was. She'd be getting out of that poetry writing class soon. Then she'd have an hour before a literature lecture. I didn't know if she'd be heading to her office or not between classes. I didn't know an hour ago if I'd try to see Ashley or just do a reconnaissance mission. But I knew now. I wanted to see her. And I was going to stand in the hallway outside her office door and hope she'd be there.

Her building was unimpressive. Some of the buildings were from the early twentieth century and were in that nice-looking mission revival. You know, rounded archways, Spanish influence but unequivocally Californian. But the humanities building was a mid-century box. Had it been taller I would have called it jail-like. Actually, I'll go ahead and call it jail-like. It was a two-story cinder block cube with narrow windows. It was painted tan to match the rest of the campus, and there were nice bougainvillea and trees and shrubs around to mask the building's plainness, but the structure itself was clearly a quick cheap fix for a lack of classrooms and office space.

So I walked down the hallway where the English professors had their offices, and no one's around and I'm looking at the placards by the doors—Dr. So-and-so, Dr. So-and-so, Dr. So-and-so—and before I see Ashley's name I hear her voice because there's an office door open down there and her sweet chirpings are echoing in the hallway, but then when I was right outside her door, I stood corrected because she sounded mad, kind of frustrated, so cross out the chirping description above—which I suppose, reflecting on it, is maybe misogynistic—and replace with the sound of regular yet hyper-educated strong woman talking sternly to what I gathered was a dipshit, rude male student. He said, "Whatever." And she said, "It's a zero in your gradebook until you redo it." And I heard him walk toward the door, and I turned my body to face the wall and played invisible, and three, four, five steps past me, he whispered, "Cunt." And the syllable kind of landed on my left cheek and ear, and I tried to keep it there by cupping my hand to my skin right away, and there was just no way of telling if it broke past me and made it into Ashley's office, but she slammed her door from inside her office, so there I was, wondering if I should give it a minute and then knock on her door and surprise her, but when I heard dipshit male student trouncing down the staircase at the end of the hall, I booked it after him.

You might think you know what's going to happen next. You might be thinking: A) Fight on the quad, or B) Joe will follow him to a secluded area and beat him appropriately. And obviously those things could have happened because I did think about them happening, but I'm also a patient person. I'm not rash. If anything I'm too slow in my thinking for most, too deliberate. Ask the most impatient of my few exes. Ask if it drove her crazy when we were in an argument and I took my time responding. Oh, she hated it. I was thinking, I don't even want to be in a fight right now. How did this happen again? And she was, Say something! Say something! Say something! So at one point or another what I said was, I guess I'm leaving now because you are way too mad for me.

But I followed this guy who called Ashley what he called her, and he took his sweet ass time getting anywhere. There he was high-fiving his buddies, there he was buying some fancy coffee concoction, there he was sitting with some girl, caressing the drooping curls of her hair like a guy who cares about women and not just this girl. And finally, finally, they got up from their spot on the grass and they walked across the parking lot and they walked to one of the student housing buildings, and so many marvelous plans went through my head, like what would be the best way to hurt this guy, so of course one thing I thought was, well, I need to follow her, and I need to befriend her and have her fall in love with me, and then I need to send this guy some evidence of me and this girl with her being in love with me and me faking it for the sake of Ashley, because, you know, what hurts more than discovering the one you love is not into you but somebody else? But I couldn't trust in my abilities to pull that off in so little time because I'm not really a Casanova-type guy, and I didn't want to scare her, so, after all this rambling, you had it right with option B above: Joe will follow him to a secluded area and beat him appropriately. And you're probably thinking, Ugh, toxic masculinity. Here we go again. What's wrong with you guys. But I can't regulate the testosterone flowing through my bloodstream, and maybe that's a poor excuse anyway, but I did what I did, so let me still tell you about it.

They kissed for a bit. And I really did wish the best for them if they were going to end up together and get married someday, have babies and all, him working as an assistant youth pastor at his childhood church while she worked nights as a labor and delivery nurse until she could finally get into the daytime rotation after X amount of years of service. So I wished the best for them, but I was still upset because of the whole Ashley incident, so when he finally walked away from his girl's building and started on the path to what must have led to his own dorm, I crept behind about thirty feet, and I opened up my backpack and pulled out Ashley's purple socks with the mixture of white polka dots and coffee-stained polka dots, and I slid each sock over a hand and up each arm till they stopped at my elbows. And right there where the path kind of curved by one of those desert-hardy trees with long, thin leaves like fingers, I ran full sprint toward him and punched him in the spine, and when he shrieked, then crumpled, I unbent him and hopped on his torso, my legs straddling either side, and he tried to block his face with his hands, but I was right punch left punch right punch left punch, and my knuckles didn't bleed because those were some good quality socks, so thick for Midwest winters, but his face bled, and I stopped at just four, because he was tender and wailing wailing wailing for his mom even though he didn't call her name because those of us who had dads for a while would never cry out for them in moments like these, and I took my socked right hand, and I smeared his blood across his smooth cheeks and forehead, and across to his ears, and down his neck and back up to his mouth, and I thought about forcing my hand into his mouth to pull on his tongue for a bit, but there! and there! some people were screaming from two stories up, and off in the distance someone was running toward us, so I ran in the other direction. And I ran until I reached the edge of campus, and I climbed a fence, hopped down, then ran and ran until I was far away, at last remembering to pull off the socks and return them to my backpack.

I walked a long loop back toward my car. I enjoyed that walk. I wished I could have seen the inside of Ashley's office. No doubt she'll hear or read about the attack in some campus security email, but I didn't worry about her suspecting me. Why would she? And I was just upset that I couldn't visit there again for a long while. And while thinking about the bad luck that I got put into that situation, I made it to my car conflict-free and drove back to Riverside. As I said, my hands weren't damaged, and I looked in my rearview mirror and saw my face was clean too, but I hadn't shaved in a while and my stubble looked thicker than it did that morning, so I drove to my barber on Main Street and treated myself to a hot shave and a trim at the edges.

IV

Swimming Boy and Snowy Girl

ONCE A SWIMMING BOY came to love a snowy girl. When he swished up to her grotto, she raised a hand and said, "Only so far, ocean boy, your salty skin will melt what I've built in there." Her words popped out as little snowflakes, alighting on his arms, his cheeks, his neck, dissolving on their glazings. He looked past the threshold and wanted to go inside. She'd built some lovely snow drifts, as well as two couches and a dinette set to seat four for a double-couple's dinner. He wanted to go inside. But he wouldn't barge in. "Will I ever be allowed in?" he asked. "Ever get to dive into your snowbanks and perhaps do the butterfly over there across that slick dinette set? Because, you know, I'd like to do that." But the snowy girl drifted mutely backwards while staring at the swimming boy. Her look was indecipherable, like a snowy owl, stoic and unchanging, and he usually liked that, but now, now he wished her look was like a common harbor seal, perpetually smiling. That look he could decipher. But the swimming boy couldn't read the snowy girl. Couldn't read her owl face there blocking her grotto. Couldn't label it *Barge in* or *Swim off* or *Still computing, read again in X amount of time.* So the swimming boy swished backward to wait for more words. The swimming boy was not a perfect boy, but his mother had taught him to wait for the right words, at least. The snowy girl glided back to where he couldn't see her, and he stayed outside, fashioning a necklace out of stray kelp and placing it before her grotto. Then he poured himself back into the ocean, gnashing the bull kelp's leaves with his molars, tearing its roots with his fingers, until he tired himself out and slept flat in the sand among the righteye flounders.

5

THEN AFTER THE socks-on-the-arms incident, I had a date with Ashley that Friday, and she said my haircut looked nice, all trimmed at the sides and slicked down on top. We walked up Mt. Rubidoux while the sun was setting, then found a semi-secluded bench to chat at for a while. We chatted about this and that. Lots of small talk. Was it always small talk with us? I don't think so. No, it wasn't. Because we talked about her family that night, and that led to some important things. We talked about her brother and sister-in-law getting pregnant. Intentionally. And how she was excited.

She'd turned to me on the bench and, out of nowhere, she said, "Dan's pregnant." And I didn't know who Dan was, and I couldn't tell if she was happy or sad about this. Actually she seemed sad. But then her expressionless face took on a smile, and she said, "My little brother Dan, and his wife Sarah, they're pregnant."

And I said, "Whoa!" I said, "That's great. Aunt Ashley. Auntie Ash. You'll be terrific."

And she said, "Thanks."

And I said, "Well, is that it? What else? More details."

"It's weird," she said. "He's only twenty-five. He got married before I did, and now this. It's not a competition, of course. But I just thought I'd do those things before him."

"Sure," I said. "Sure."

"He and Sarah got married at twenty-two. Fresh out of college. And they're the perfect couple. All loving and polite all the time. And when they were engaged a short while and then got married super quick, one thing I kept thinking was, my little brother will celebrate all his wedding anniversaries before me. He'll reach twenty-five years and fifty years before I do, and I know that was self-centered of me, but I was thinking things like that. And now he'll have all the baby milestones before I do. And his kid will graduate from high school and college before my firstborn does. Anyway. Selfish, ridiculous thoughts."

"They're not," I said. "Those are natural reactions. You're a human being. You're not selfish. You're just human. And who cares about who gets to fifty years? Does anyone get there anymore? Does it matter? That could be a bad motivation for staying in a marriage. Anyway, you're not wrong for thinking those thoughts, that's all."

"Thanks," she said. And then she grinned at me and said, "I'm getting to fifty and then some. I don't know about you," she said. "But I'm getting there."

"Sounds good," I said. "I'll take fifty years with the right person, but I'm not sticking around with the wrong person just to brag about a milestone." And I thought I should shift the conversation and not be a downer and not let it slip that I'd spent so many years of my childhood hearing my parents yell at each other that I couldn't possibly have anything other than a realistic viewpoint on the matter. So I said, "And how many kids will you and Mr. Fifty-Plus-Years be having."

And she smirked and did this sexy narrowing of the eyes thing that maybe wasn't supposed to be sexy? but come on, it was, and she said, "Two to five. Actually? Two to three. But maybe four under the right conditions—age, incomes, local schools good enough or needing to do private." She was so serious now. Boy, had she thought about this. "Yes," she said. "Anywhere from two to four."

"Okay," I said. "You've got a plan," I said.

And then she asked me too, saying, "All right, mister. What's your number? How many kids?"

And I said, "Well, doctor, I haven't thought about that much in my life. Maybe this morning I would have said zero to one, or maybe zero to two, but now, now in this glimmering dusk, I'm thinking two to four sounds about right."

And she leaned in and kissed me. And she said, "That was cute." And then she said, "We should head down the path. Do you want dinner or just coffee? I'm not too hungry myself."

I said, "How about a swim? Drive to the ocean, run across the sand, and just dive in. I know a great little spot right where Seal Beach and Sunset meet."

She said, "Oh man, well, I wish I could be that daring." She said, "But maybe next time. Definitely another time."

We had coffee and these killer cinnamon rolls not far from where I worked. Different café. More of a hipster hangout, which isn't my thing, but I didn't mind it because Ashley was happy. And then we went back to her place, and we kissed for a while like we do, and she fell asleep on the couch while we were watching

Alice through the Looking Glass, which had just come out on DVD, and it was kind of a bust but pretty to look at, and her legs were stretched across me, and I thought about carrying her to her bed over there, but I let her sleep while I finished the movie, and I caressed her legs from ankle to knee, not creepily, just like a normal boyfriend, just a normal caress, and if I could have gotten away with it, I would have licked her calf or her shin, just because it seemed nice, and that's something, and little things can sustain, but I was kind of trapped, so I just sat there, and then it was weird because as soon as the movie ended and the credits ended and there was no sound whatsoever, she stood up and kept her eyes closed, just stood up and walked over to her bed from memory, sleepwalking her way and slipping under the covers in her clothes.

"Good night," I said, just to say it, even though I didn't think she would respond.

But she mumbled something about pancakes and the wind in Chicago, and then I turned everything off and grabbed her keys off the counter. The stove clock said 11:37 a.m. I locked her doorknob and deadbolt on my way out. I wasn't tired and needed to walk a mile or two in the cool air before I'd be able to sleep.

Ashley lived near downtown, so I walked that way. I ended up on Main Street where the quaint shops were, and then the Mission Inn slapped my eyes, sticking out all prominent and sure of itself. It's kind of a crazy hotel, like a big monastery, or I guess a mission, but it was never actually used for that, just looks like it, with its big arches and bells, and its domes and spires. Are those spires?—the pointy deals along the long roof. And I've walked around the hotel before even though you're supposed to be a hotel guest past the lobby and restaurants. And once you're inside walking around, it feels like I imagine much of Europe to be like. Think of travel magazines: bougainvillea exploding with pink flowers throughout courtyards, sturdy wood furniture, wrought-iron furniture, high ceilings, little fountains, long pergolas with vines. Think of the feeling of being inside and outside at the same time, and, of course, think of there being more beautiful people than un-beautiful people, all of them looking like they have money and things, all of them eager for athletic hotel sex, even those on the pudgy side, because, hey, it's vacation.

I made it to the bar inside the lobby, took a seat and ordered a porter because I like my beer as dark as possible. It was called The Presidential Lounge. I think perhaps some presidents have stayed at the hotel or had drinks here. The beer was good. I drank it while looking around. Other people, I've noticed, when they're alone like I was, they need their phone out. They need to seem engaged with something, like they're not really alone at all. Not me. I don't mind being alone. Prefer it, actually, except that I still want to be with Ashley and see some people now and again. I mean I don't want to be a hermit or a recluse or anything like that by choice. I just prefer being alone about 70 percent of the time. I think if I was alone-alone, I would go crazy eventually.

But I liked being alone there at the bar in that moment, and I didn't mind my aloneness being on display. I drank my beer and observed. And then I ordered a second. I watched the couples who were still out on dates, and I watched groups of friends out drinking together after dinners or other gatherings.

And then there she was. My most recent ex from a couple years back. Really I'd only had two serious girlfriends in my life before dating Ashley. One was from college, and one was after college. This was the after-college one. Cora. Super talkative. Loud really, especially when she'd been drinking. And I liked that about her. Some people get sad when they drink, all depressed; others get mean, like all their resentment spills out of them because of the booze. Forget that. I don't like being around either of those people. Cora was a happy drunk, and those are the best kind. That girl was all passion and friendliness. And I could tell my quietness bothered her sometimes even though I was glad she never said so. And is it surprising that I was the one to break it off with her? Because I did. I could just tell we were a mismatch, and I broke up with her because she deserved someone better but also she had her own issues I wasn't equipped to handle. I'd been having regressions in dealing with Mom's death and was wondering if maybe my dad was out there in the world, and I'd graduated college without any kind of purpose, and those are things that don't bother me anymore, but, I don't know, at the time I was struggling but couldn't open up about anything, and maybe if I'd had a therapist and a prescription, I could have been an amazing boyfriend/husband to Cora for decades to come because I loved being around her even though sometimes she was a tad too bubbly, and in a night after we'd been together and were in her bed sleeping, I just got up and wrote a note saying:

I love you so much, but you maybe need a guy named Chad who can bobble his head at the same pace as you and whose cheeks don't tire from smiling smiling smiling all the time. I'm tired. My cheeks, my mouth, my eyebrows. I'm just tired. But I love you. Oh how I love you. But I don't love that I saw you pulling out pieces of your hair in what you must have thought was a private moment in the shower earlier tonight? Because I had to pee, and you were in there, and the curtain was barely slid closed, and I saw you pull pull pull and the blood and water mixing at your feet. But then when you came out and joined me in bed, you were your regular bouncy self, and you smiled, and I smiled, and you smiled, and I smiled. But I'm tired and you deserve so much more. Like lollipops and maybe someone who can buy a newish car and likes to go rollerblading with his nephews and nieces and cousins on a shady afternoon in June. And you deserve items of significance and I'm rambling now. Just remember I love you and that life can be aces.

And by the time I'd finished writing it, I didn't remember it being a break-up note per se. But I left and either walked home or drove home, and then when I called Cora the next day and she was acting like I'd broken up with her, I was confused, and she read me that note, and I said, "Well, I'd been drinking." And she said, "Doesn't matter. Still counts." And that was the last time I'd talked to her some years back, and I regretted it, and I missed her, and I tried a couple more times to patch things up, leaving texts and voicemails, but she was set on accepting my break-up, and then I got over it eventually and didn't mind being without her at all. Because we can get over anyone, can't we? And we can be happy with so many different people, right? It's just dumb luck and other circumstances dictating which of the many potential matches we settle down with, yes? So the brain was saying. So the brain was saying. But the heart said, Hogwash. The heart said, Ashley Ashley Ashley.

And then Cora spotted me sitting there, and she gave a look like, No Fucking Way. This big smile and this head shake. And she stood up, and she marched over to my stool. She's short and is real shapely and has blonde curly hair and freckles on her nose, and she grabbed my arm and tugged me, and I managed to grab my beer with my free hand, and she kept pulling me until I was thrown into her table with these three other folks.

Cora said, "Joe, I'd like you to meet *Chad*. Chad, this is my ex, Joe."

And her friends looked at her like she was wonky, and I smelled the gin, and I held out my hand to Chad, but Chad said, "Babe, you're crazy." And he shook my hand and said, "It's Dale. My name's Dale. Nice to meet you. Actually no, it's not. What the hell did you drag him over here for. Your ex? This is ridiculous."

"It's an inside joke," she said. "Relax, hon. Shit. Just relax, everybody."

So there I was sandwiched between Cora and Chad/Dale. And across the table on the other bench was this couple I didn't know. But you know what? I had nothing to lose. What did I care? I had my girl Ashley asleep back home. I was happy. I was in a good place. I could hang out with these people and they could love me or hate me. I was just killing time.

I sipped my beer. I said to the couple across from me, "Hi. I'm Joe. You guys having a good night?"

And the gal said, "Melissa. Nice to meet you."

And the guy said, "Pedro. Nice to meet you." And then he said, "Yeah, we're having a good time. It's our first date. Dale introduced us. It's been a great time."

And Melissa echoed that. She looked sweet-like at this guy Pedro and said, "Yeah, it's been really great."

"Swell," I said. "Swell times. Here's what I'm going to do. I'm going to go back to my stool and finish this beer, and I'm going to order a round for the four of you and have it sent over. On me. Because I love you guys. Actually I don't love all of you. I love you Melissa and Pedro because you seem like good folk. And I love you Cora because I always will despite everything. But I don't love you Chad." And I turned to him and said this right in his face because I wanted to see what would happen. Just to see. I said, "I don't love you Chad or Dale or whatever your name is. Because from the few words I've heard from you, you seem like a jackass. But I'll still buy you a drink. Because I don't envy you. I don't envy you studying my face right now. Looking at my mouth and the size of my hands and imagining what life was like when Cora and I were together."

And I wondered if he would hit me. I was inches from his face. And what the hell happened to me? I don't know. I'm a nice guy. A good guy. And this poor guy was on the brink of tears. So I stood awkwardly, and then I gently nudged Cora to let me slip out of the bench, and she did, and then she slapped me hard. And I grabbed my beer and drank the rest and then set the glass on their table. I said, "Melissa and Pedro, your next date should be just you guys, I think." And I said, "Cora, we'd probably be pretty happy together right now if a drunken note could just be a drunken note. But maybe I'm wrong. Anyway, here's to hoping we can do better." And I did an imaginary raise of my glass. And I said, "By the looks of it, I'm a few steps ahead of you in that department."

And I walked to the bar, and Chad/Dale whispered, "Asshole," but I chose not to turn around.

And I asked the bartender what the froofiest drink they had was. And she said, "You mean something with fruit?"

And I said, "Yeah, something elaborate. Bells and whistles." And she handed me a drink list and pointed to a few cocktails. And there wasn't anything too fancy like I'd hoped. So I ordered them three gin-and-tonics and a coconut rum drink. And I said, "The coconut one is for that guy," pointing to Chad/Dale. And I ordered myself two shots of the well whiskey, and I drank those real quick instead of a third beer, and I ventured back into the hotel lobby as the drinks were being delivered.

The lobby of the Mission Inn is a magical place. At least it is to me since I don't get out much. I mean traveling to other high-class hotels. I was going to leave the lobby and walk out into the coolness. I was going to walk back to Ashley's, maybe even walk to the river, maybe even walk down into the dried-up riverbed if I was brave enough, get a taste of tent life at night, hear what I could hear. But they're all addicts down there aside from one or two seemingly clean crazies like Ronnie, and it's a sad scene when you think about it. From what I'd heard, heroin was the main drug down there in the river bottom, but I didn't know for sure. All I knew then was I didn't want to walk around in the cool night and be brought down by so much sadness, even though part of me was curious to peek in on that underworld.

In the lobby, they've got different sitting areas, nice comfy chairs with high backs placed around fireplaces and tables with fancy vases and lamps. I took a seat across from The Presidential Lounge. I wanted to see when that foursome would head out. I'd been a dick to that guy, and he probably didn't deserve it. He was skinny but you should never underestimate people. And people can be bonkers. Skinny guys can hide strong guns. Skinny guys can strap knives to their calves. But not that guy. He was just some person my ex was dating. Who knows for how long? I decided sitting there that if he came out and saw me and wanted to fight me, I'd go out with him to an alley a block over and let him have at it. I'd stand there and let him wail on me for as long as I could keep my legs under me. Then I'd collapse to the pavement and cradle my head, letting him kick out his life's disappointments until he felt it was time to walk away. I could give him that, at least.

But Cora's new boyfriend didn't come out first. First it was that sweet couple Melissa and Pedro. They came out of the bar's opening hand-in-hand. What lovely red boots she had. His jeans were tight but I didn't fault him for that. His hair was dark like mine, hers a light brown with waves. I was rooting for them. Not that they cared what I thought or hoped. They saw me, and I waved, and I gave them a thumbs-up and pointed with two hands kind of playful-like. I don't do things like that, so I guess the booze was working on me since I hadn't eaten enough when I was out with Ashley. They waved and kept walking and exited the door and went out into the night to conclude their evening somehow. In my head I said, God, watch over those two and give them happiness. Happiness with each other. Or with others if they're not a good fit. But not so much happiness as fulfillment. God, help those two feel fulfilled in their lives somehow. And while I was praying that, Cora's boyfriend Dale walked out of the bar, and he looked left, and he looked right, and then he went that way toward the exit on Orange Street, the opposite direction of Melissa and Pedro, and he went through the glass doors by himself and turned the corner.

Sitting there, I wondered what to do about Cora. Do I go back into the bar and comfort her? Apologize for my behavior even though she was the one who dragged me over to her group in the first place? Or should I just stay seated in this comfy, classy chair, all distinguished in this lovely lobby? I didn't know. So I sat for a few more minutes. The lobby was still pretty active despite it being about 1:00 a.m. Some people were even checking in with luggage, but most of the folks around were spilling out into the night from the bar or restaurants or else coming back to their rooms from being out downtown. Then Cora emerged and she looked real beautiful pausing just outside the entrance/exit, standing there kind of thinking about what her next move should be. I stood. I stood and took a step toward her, hands in my pockets. She saw me then. She saw me then and walked over to me. She had a confident step, and her face was serious, her lip line straight when it's almost always curved up. She sidled next to me and slipped her arm through mine. We headed for the nearest exit, interlocked, steps in unison even though my legs are twice as long as hers, instinctively, like people comfortable with each other, like people settling into each other who have had enough of uncertainty.

I said, "Do you have your car?"

And she said, "He drove."

So I said, "Same place?"

And she said, "Yeah." So we walked to her place like that, and it was about a twenty-minute walk to Eastside, where her apartment was, down University toward UC Riverside but not that far, and she didn't live in the best neighborhood but her complex was really nice; she'd studied art and painting at UCR and never left the area even though her parents used to beg her to move back north to their small town outside Sacramento.

We made it to her place, arms still interlocked, not having said a word between us. And she unlocked her door, and we stepped in together, like partners at a picnic in a three-legged race. And I said, "You good?" And she squared off in front of me, and I thought she was going to smack me again, but she craned her neck up to kiss me, and I pulled away and said, "I'm with someone."

She closed the door and said, "So?" She edged me to the wall and said, "I was wrong. We could have kept going."

"Maybe not," I said. "It doesn't matter now," I said.

And she tried to kiss me a second time, and again I moved my head away, and then she said, "Fine." And she hugged me, just holding onto me, and I was pinned against the wall, right next to the door, and I held onto her, and I let her hold onto me, and she pushed her face into my chest, and still I held her and gave her this moment, and my shirt was absorbing her tears, and I kissed the top of her head—just to be compassionate, just to be a good person in this moment—and she kept her face pressed into my chest, and she unlocked an arm from around me, and she pushed a hand beneath my belt and her hand maneuvered around inside my pants, and it gripped me and it moved slowly, carefully like it knew it should, like it used to, and I was staring at the ceiling, and my chest felt her hot breath through my shirt, and I didn't look down at her, and I didn't stop her, and we stayed like that until it was over. And when it was over, she unwrapped her other arm from around my waist, and she separated from me and washed her hands in the kitchen sink and went to the couch and plopped onto her stomach.

I stood with my back against the wall. I watched her body breathe up and down. The microwave clock said 2:32 a.m. I opened the door, locked the handle, and closed it. I walked down her street. I walked back through downtown. I walked to Ashley's place. I pulled Ashley's keys out of my pocket and went inside. I splashed water on my face. I kicked off my shoes and tucked them against a wall. I hovered over Ashley. I could scream, I thought. I could weep, I thought. But all I did was find my way to the couch, thinking, thinking, while staring at the ceiling. And I pinched myself, and I said, "Mind, don't you leave this body."

I've often thought we'd all be better people if we imagined we were being watched over by someone or something other than God, some lesser form, an angel or a dead family member, watching our performances throughout the day, watching us trying to do our best. But I don't think dead family members and friends have the option of looking down to earth—what a terrible afterlife that would be, right? You're supposed to be in infinite joy, but hey, why not glimpse down at all this pain and ineptitude every once in a while? No, I don't buy it. And I don't know about angels rooting for us or protecting us or caring if we screw up or do well. The only one watching us is God, and God forgives, and God's seen worse than this, and if God can forgive David, then I'm not hopeless, but what to tell Ashley? What to tell Ashley, if anything? What, if anything?

V

A Person Newly Angeled

ONCE. ONCE. ONCE. Then the person newly angeled peered over her cloud. One might compare her to a kid peering over a hotel balcony to check out the pool, gripping the cool metal and delighting in the strangeness and danger and privilege of the angle, but there's no need to do that: The newly angeled person gripped cloud wisps like a newly angeled person. She stretched her peering self. She squinted. She located him right away, him down there, her former husband, scraping cheek along asphalt, crawling somewhere on knees and elbows and sometimes face, a face seeming too heavy for that neck?

"He looks silly," she said.

"He is," said a voice.

Whose voice? Who knew? She didn't know yet. She knew it was a voice. She wondered if she should feel non-happy about all this. "Is something lingering?" she asked. "Like maybe I shouldn't think he looks so silly with those pebbles in that open wound while he is— what is that?—is he flipping over?—backstroking in that rock garden when breaststroking would work better or—of course!—walking."

A voice said, "You'll stop looking soon. You'll look out and not down. You'll look up, too, but out comes first. You can't feel unhappy watching down. But you can't feel happy either."

The person newly angeled said, "Ok." The person newly angeled asked, "Can I park it here for a while? Watching over that silly man?"

The voice was silent or absent, so she scanned the terrain past her former someone, and the asphalt gave way to weeds and wheat stalks. Weren't there other things there? She remembered something about things, maybe?—things with tops to them?—coverings?—maybe carousels in which to habituate for a spell?

Then her eyes dipped back to her him, but he was a wheat stalk, not a person. But was that even him? And was he a him? Or was he an it? Of course! Her lovely wheat stalk! Such a prominent wheat stalk shooting up like that. She'd always tingled at its kernels, hadn't she? Or was that her precious stalk over there? Yes, that one. And that one, too. And were there once other things among these wheat stalks? No, she didn't think there were. The field was all wheat stalk wherever one peered. She marveled at the field below for days or maybe seconds. Such wonders, those wheat stalks. Rows and rows of them and nothing else. Swimming in the breeze a bit here, then a bit there. But she grew tired of their dull wonder and gazed elsewhere.

6

IN THE WEEKS when Ronnie's elbow was healing, sometimes he'd call and sometimes I'd answer. He'd ask for rides to the grocery store every few days, just until his elbow had healed up and he could ride his bike again. I'd already seen him riding his bike around town, but sometimes I'd say, Sure. Sometimes I'd drive over and get him so he could pick up more dog food and people food, as he'd say.

On the way back from one of our grocery-store runs, he said this—I didn't ask him a question, didn't prompt him in any way—he just said this: "When you sleep in the shelter, man, they get your ass up early. 6:00 a.m. on the dot. I get up early as it is, but I don't like people waking me up, don't like people telling me when I need to get out of bed, you know. But you've probably never slept in a shelter. Well, they get you up and out at 6:00 a.m., and you shower at night, not in the morning. They won't let you shower in the morning. But they make you shower at night, after dinner and before bed. Here's how it works, man. Just so you know. I hate it there. You probably guessed that since I've got my camp. But sometimes I have to stay there. Like if we get those heavy rains. Did I tell you about that one time? That time with the chopper? What happened the last time I stayed there was this. I got pissed on, man. Can you believe that? Pissed on. And the bastards in charge wouldn't give me a shower.

"Picture this. Here's how it happened. Here's the story. At 6:00 a.m. some jerkoff flips on the light switch and the room goes from black to bright just like that. You know those ceilings with all the long tubes, the fluorescent lights I mean. Yeah, well, they've got those. And where the beds are is a big open room, no windows, totally black at night. Sometimes the gays cuddle up together in the bunks. Can you believe that, man? Gays bunking up in the shelter. Oh I'm telling you it happens. But not me, man. No way, man. I always grab a top bunk. But the last time I was there, man, I got stuck with a bottom bunk. And they were at full capacity on account of the rains. But I was beat, exhausted, and I conked out just fine. Henry was with Ace. Did I mention that? Whenever I have to sleep at the shelter, Henry gets to stay with Ace and Buck. Buck's his dog. Oh you know. You met him. I don't know where Ace's house is. Ace just drives to the parking lot and picks up Henry and then tells me to be safe. Safe? I say to him. Safe from what? Danger gave up on me, man. I live the safest life there is. But here's the story. At 6:00 a.m. the short guy holding the bullhorn clicks on the lights and it's instant brightness. You know, pitch black and then bam! bright tube lights stretched across the whole ceiling. Bam! darkness, then light! And he yells into his bullhorn, telling us to get up and gather our things. And that's how it works. You've got to check in by 6:00 p.m. to get a bed, and then you've got to listen to a sermon before they serve you dinner, and then after you eat you have to take a shower, and then you dry off, put your dirty clothes back on and get into bed. And then 6:00 a.m. and bullhorn guy.

"But on this morning, I woke up feeling wet. Man, I got pissed on. I was on a bottom bunk, and they've got those old thin mattresses on springs. And bullhorn guy is yelling at us to get up and out, and there's the brightness and all, but then I felt that I was wet. My chest and stomach was all wet. And I see above me that the thin mattress has a big round wet spot in the middle. And I shot up and yelled, Fuck, I got pissed on! And whatever asshole was sleeping above me was already up and out of there. Didn't even see the fucker. And I went over to bullhorn guy and said, I need a shower. Some asshole pissed on me. And he said, Showers at night only. And I bickered with him, man. But he kept his policy. And man, I wanted a shower. And normally I hate showering in that place. Normally I can't stand it because they line us up after dinner. And we march to their orders. In a line, marching to where the showers are. And there are like six showers in one open tiled area. Like a high school gym. Did you play sports, man? I did. And there's this line of guys, like forty, fifty maybe, a line of us, and we had to get naked and stack our clothes, and we stand waiting for a shower while guys cluster in there.

"And the shelter folk, the Christian folk, they watch over all this so there's no hanky panky in the showers. But it's embarrassing, you know, all of us waiting with our dicks out, sharing soap. But it's good for the ones who need the shower. But I already know how to clean myself at the river, man. And I use fresh water from the jugs. Fill them up daily at the park. But they made me leave there without a shower, and I was piss-soaked, but on account of the thunderstorm the night before, the river was higher. So I bolted from the shelter and went straight back to the river and had a swim. Threw the damn shirt away. Went for a swim naked in the Santa Ana. Normally the damn thing's so shallow you can't swim. But let me tell you, man, I was doing laps. Diving down to the bottom. New water in a dirty river. Washed that asshole's piss clean off me."

When he was done with that story, I'd already pulled my car into the dirt lot near his river-bottom entrance. I'd left the AC on while he was talking. Then when he was finished, I cut the engine and we hauled his bags down to his tent. I never asked him how he had money for groceries, and he never volunteered that info. I assumed he had to be living off more than what he got from recycling cans. But maybe that was enough. I never asked him how he had a cell phone either, but once he told me, "Obama gave me this phone, man. Obama gave us phones. Did you know that?" And he was holding out his old-style flip phone like some prized possession.

7

ONE DAY AT WORK my coworker said, "Shit. Shit. No way." She had her phone out instead of making an Americano for some guy in overalls.

I'd been looking at the guy, thinking, Overalls? No way! Classic. Way to go, you. You're doing it. Pulling it off. Faded white-blue denim. I had a smaller pair of those when I was eight. So Nineties of you.

And those were my thoughts when my coworker said, "Shit. Shit. No way."

So I turned to the guy and said, "Those look so cozy. Making me nostalgic. I'm serious. I like them." And I said, "Your Americano will be up in a minute. Take a seat and I'll bring it to you."

And he said, "Thanks." And he smiled and turned to sit.

Then I walked over to my coworker and said, "What's no way?"

And she pointed to her phone, which was propped up against the espresso machine, and she packed the espresso for the Americano and twisted the handle into the machine and said, "That's the dumpster behind my complex. Disturbing."

There was a photo of a dead goat, its hair dyed or painted light green, its tongue out, one eye open with a fly on it. The goat had a St. Patrick's Day hat on, emerald green, its horns poking through the cheap plastic.

"Who parties with a goat?" she asked. "Tragic. Tragic," she said.

"Terrible," I said. And I meant it. And I asked, "Who sent you that, anyway?"

And she said it was from her NeighborhoodConnect app. She scrolled up, and the headline read, "Dead PARTY GOAT In Dumpster Behind Paradise Apts." Then she hit back and there were so many headlines. "Man keeps Walking through our Yard." "LOST yorkie (black and white and tan and kind of orangish) answers to PRINCESS." "Homeless women peed in my bird bath." "Suspicious Person & Items." "POSSIBLE STRAYS? MAYBE MISSING CATS?" "Today around 6 p.m. a young obese woman rang my doorbell."

"Those are some stories," I said.

"People are crazy," she said.

"People are something else," I said. "They're something else. I keep reading everywhere that stories make us empathetic. That's what they say. Knowing people's stories helps us be nicer to them. Or to other people. Like what's the story behind the person not wanting to open her door to a young obese woman? Open the door and ask her what she's doing there. Simple. But she doesn't do it. Is she scared? Did she have a bad experience? I'd like to know. Or maybe it's some dude not opening his door? He should open it. Why doesn't he?"

My coworker said I should read the post later.

I said I would.

Then she handed me the Americano, and I brought it to overalls.

He said, "Thanks."

I said, "Of course."

And then after my shift I went home and I joined NeighborhoodConnect, and my email was verified, and my cell phone was verified, and I was assigned a NeighborlyCommunity based on my address and zip code, and I read peoples' stories and I read the commenters' comments, and I said, "I'd like to post something." And I answered, "You should."

Appendix A to Chapter 7

Recently Adopted Dog Lost Near Mt. Rubidoux

Hi neighbors!

I lost my recently adopted dog outside the Carlson Bark Park.

I did not mean to lose him. But he was a new dog to me and did not always respond to me. So he ran away. He answers to "Stevie." He might respond to "Steve." He is a medium-sized dog. Somewhat large. But also somewhat small.

He looks like a dog. He is brown or tan or white with some shading.

I don't fully remember because our time together was too short.

Did you find him? Are you keeping him safe? Please contact me because we had a thing going.

But also, do you have a thing going with him? Is he blending into your crew?

Then thank you for caring for him. And please keep him if all is jiving.

Or if he is still missing. Please find him and care for him. Please, if you're reading this, go take a walk outside and look for him.

He might not remember that his name is "Stevie." If a nice tan or brown or white dog (or was he grayish even?) finds you, then that's the one. Take him in and care for him.

Or was my newly adopted then lost dog a girl? Did I give a girl dog the name "Stevie?"

I might have. But really that is not so bizarre. Perhaps, thoughtful neighbor, you have heard of the late great Stevie Nicks? The voice of an angel. And two boy names. One of which is plural. I digress. Please go out and find this dog and care for it.

Please share this post far and wide.

COMMENTS

Neighbor 17

I sincerely hope your Stevie finds his way home. Don't loose hope. Seven years ago two of my dachshund mixes ran away. Oh how I searched and searched and searched for my babies. I never found them. Exactly one year after they went missing one of them just showed up. He found me. Scrawny and dirty, and a little taller, and a little yellower. But home!

Neighbor 22

So sad when this happens. Good luck to you. Neighbor 17, such a heartwarming story.

Neighbor 57

You didnt give your number? How can I reach you if I see him. I mean her. I mean your dog???

Poster

If you see my dog, respond here ASAP with a full description. I will let you know if you have found my dog or your future dog. Go now! Look!

Neighbor 32

Is this a joke?

Poster

Searching for and caring for and thinking about lonely animals in need is never a joke. And please be more sensitive. I am still mourning this new absence.

Neighbor 32

Your right. And I'm so sorry. And I am sensitive BTW

Neighbor 89

Stevie Nicks isn't dead. And her birthname is Stephanie. Did you mean "late" as in tardy, or are you deft?

Poster

I AM deft. Of course I meant tardy. Don't be daft. And have you found your dog yet, Neighbor 89?

COMMENTS CLOSED

Appendix B to Chapter 7

At-Risk Missing Person with Alzheimer's

ESTHER SHRINESEEKER

+ 77 years old

+ Female, 5'2" tall, 112 lbs., golden-skinned, black hair with silver streaks, brown eyes

+ Last seen wearing a gray blouse with ribbons, blue jeans, white crocs, multiple turquoise bracelets. She might have put on her silver tiara (plastic with glass jewels), and she might be carrying a large white handbag with lemon prints (the handbag is empty unless she did not put on her tiara, in which case the handbag has only a plastic tiara in it, nothing of value)

+ Suffers from advanced Alzheimer's

Esther Shrineseeker has been reported missing today—Sunday, March 19, 2017—after getting out of her wheelchair and exiting the 10:00 a.m. service at the First United Methodist Church of Riverside, located at 4845 Brockton Avenue. Her family did not notice her walk out of the service because they were engrossed in the sermon. Her family is worried about her. They ask that everyone be on the lookout for her and all elderly in need. She may be disoriented. Please approach her or any elderly individual slowly and with great kindness. Use nice words like, "Hello." And, "May I help you." And, "Do you require assistance?" Or, "Can I buy that pomegranate for you? Or that garden hose draped on your shoulder?"

If you have seen Ms. Shrineseeker or know of her whereabouts, please call the Public Safety line. The family urges: please approach her and all people with extreme kindness.

Comments

Neighbor 27

I sure hope Miss Esther finds her way back home. May I suggest some kind of tether device to keep her from getting out of her chair unsupervised?? A loose tether of course. I will keep my eyes peeled. I will be praying for her and you and all of our neighbors.

Neighbor 22

So sad when this happens. Good luck to you.

Neighbor 11

Arent these normally posted by the police with an official phone number? Where is the phone number? Take for example this situation. I just read your post on my phone and I am currently in the process of typing this response. Well guess what? By chance or good fortune I am about three blocks from the church you post of. Near RCC. What if right now. THIS VERY SECOND! I saw her in her white crocs exsetera and I cant call you because there is no number. Would me spotting her warrant a call to 911?? I'm not sure. Because I have once gotten chewed out by a dispatch person for using the number in a non emergency type situation. Do I want to risk that? I might. This is for your sweet nana after all. But did you recognize the delay. Thats the key takeaway for you poster. The delay. Dont risk it. Put down the number. Oh heres my bus. Good luck. She is not at this moment at the bus stop near RCC.

Neighbor 32

Is this a joke?

Poster

Searching for and caring for and thinking about lonely elderly in need is never a joke. Please be more sensitive to those of us with an absence.

Neighbor 32

That's true. You sound like someone I know. Or maybe it's that wise words sound familiar?

Neighbor 91

So sad when this kind of thing happens.

Poster

Update: While Esther Shrineseeker remains unfound, multiple people in these vicinities [zip codes 92509, 92501, 92506] have reported instances of having been approached by concerned citizens with extreme kindness, being asked if they are ok and in need of fruit and/or direction. Well done! Keep it up!

Comments Closed

8

I'M A FIRM BELIEVER in bus riding, especially if you own a car. Don't get me wrong. I'm not up in my pulpit preaching about the environment. I guess I do that sometimes. But the thing about bus riding is the orientation, the way it reminds you of your place. Because, well, consider the people. No, I mean, consider yourself. First, consider yourself. You probably think people are: A) generally amazing or B) generally terrible. Or maybe now you're thinking, Oh, Joe, really? Binaries? Are you that limited in perception? Do you really think I'm choosing A or B? Obviously people are C): generally in that gray area between amazing and terrible. And this is where I need to correct you because this has nothing to do with binaries or gray areas. There's only one thing here. Just one thing. People are amazing. Just super amazing.

There I was this morning riding the bus. Ashley was working, and I had the day off, and I decided to wander out of my apartment and ride the bus to goodness-knows-where. So I was riding the bus. And in the past I've struck up conversations with people, and I've learned about Harold, who works at the Old Spaghetti Factory but is good in his biology class and wants to be a veterinarian but is squeamish about the idea of slicing open animals and then stitching them up, not to mention attending to their inner parts between all that, and I said, "Harold, you're a good kid with a good head. The slicing will come when you see it as an act of grace"—and I've learned about Katherine, who was worried about whether to change her braces' color from lavender, which she called a safe choice, to rainbow-patterned, which she called bold but said could look super-cool since no one in her seventh-grade class had done that yet as far as she knew, and I said, "Be bold. You're wonderful, and it will look amazing whether or not everyone says so," and her mother, sitting on her other side, gave me the look that says, It's time to stop talking to my daughter, so I pulled the cord and exited at the next stop because I didn't want to worry her and overstep my bounds as their traveling companion. And also in the past I've decided to follow people.

Not in a creepy way. But just as a kind of protector. Just in case. Like I would study the bus riders, and I would think to myself, If anyone was going to get mugged today, who would it be? Because of course that happens to undeserving people. And we read about things like that in the paper or see them on the news. So what if we made ourselves a bit more available? Just available to be around in case we stop something from happening to someone who shouldn't have something happen to them. And I can hear the objections. But no, no, no. I'm not talking about chivalry. Chivalry was stupid, misguided. That's not what I'm talking about. But isn't it true that perhaps I can help someone in need who doesn't share my stature, et cetera? Boy or girl. Man or woman.

One time, for example, I followed a boy down the sidewalk because for some reason I just feared that he was about to be a lad in distress. He was ten, eleven, maybe twelve, and I followed him multiple blocks and then noticed that this other guy was also following him, so I stayed near the other guy, ready to swoop in if it came to that, but then the guy changed direction and the boy eventually stopped in front of the post office and met up with a young mother or an older sister or perhaps an aunt, and they hugged, and she tousled his hair, and I smiled at the tender moment, but the young woman looked at me like, Get your ass out of here, weirdo. But I wanted to say, Hey, I'm on your side. But instead, I just kept walking, content that my meanderings so often let me witness more kindnesses than harms.

But today I was on the bus and listened to this lady tell me about the book she was going to write. Here's the story:

I had the day off, et cetera. Ashley was working, et cetera. I decided to ride the bus and get lost somewhere, then take a long walk back. I sat toward the front, so I was facing the aisle, and there were two people across from me, an older guy, sixties probably, reading the paper, and a guy just older than me, thirties I'd guess, reading his phone. It was early, but not many people seemed headed to work yet. I looked out the window for a while. The world was moving along like it does. The world was concrete. The world was steel. The ugliest rubble when the world must cease eventually. The most beautiful dust, not counting our bodies or the bodies of animals and plants—the most beautiful dust will be the seaside mansions that crumble and corrode and shine like jagged crystals before being blown away by the wind. But there! a flash: a blue egg in a nest of hair. And the mind wonders, a barrette? Or, perhaps, that was a tree and not a woman. And there! a giant red apple floating beside a pillar of fire, both burning the gray morning. But, of course, the bus stopped, and clarity extinguishing the burning apple was a disappointment, but also then a glorious woman in an orange jogging suit boarded the bus and sat beside me even though there were plenty of spare seats not next to me, and I liked this act of connection on her part, so I said, "Hello."

She said, "Thank you for saying hi to me."

I said, "Of course." I said, "Thank you for sitting next to me."

"I have a son who looks like you," she said. "He looks like he is from no-where and everywhere. Did you know you look like that?"

I shook my head no.

She said, "Timeless, I guess. And also, nondescript. Is that the right word? Nondescript?"

"It sounds like the right word to me."

"It means you might be right out of a time machine. But you dress plain and keep your hair neat, so really, who knows? Who knows where you're from or what you're up to?"

"I like your orange jumpsuit."

"It's comfortable."

"It's descript," I said.

"You're funny," she said. "I bet you have stories," she said. She said, "I have stories."

"Get them down," I said. "The world might need them. I've been sitting here thinking about chasing the wind. And it saddens me, but maybe your sto-ries will make everything okay for someone. Do you know what I mean? We just don't ever know."

"I have the dragon software. Have you heard of it?"

I shook my head no.

"It's voice recording. I have the disc. My son's going to install it on my computer one day. Then I can say aloud my story. Then I can write my book by speaking my book. Have you heard of that? I have the disc. It's the dragon program. In a box from a few Christmases ago. Because then I can make my book by saying it all out loud. It types it all for you. Just like that."

"Sounds magical," I said. "Sounds like you've got a plan," I said.

She said, "You just wait. It's going to be something." The bus slowed, and she stood. Then she said, "There's a good buy on honey crisps today. Buy them while they're cheap and put them in the fridge."

"Ok," I said. "You have a nice day," I said. "Do you need help shopping? I have time."

"Don't be crazy," she said. "I can get my crisps."

She left the bus, and as she crossed the street toward the market, I breathed out a prayer that she would not get hit by a car today or any day and that she would find the most dent-free honey crisps in the batch and that they would taste sweeter than anything she has ever tasted, and I prayed that her son would be more than a decent son to her before she died somehow at some time and that while she's here on earth she might know more joys than hardships. And then I rode for a few more uneventful exits and walked back home.

VI

The Found Story of Guy Nielson, Last Saved 3/31/2017 10:14 p.m.

Welcome to a new document for your Chameleon Voice Recognition Software, Premiere Version 2.0. You can delete these instructions anytime or you can keep them for reference while working on your document. This greeting will appear in each document opened when your Chameleon toolbar is on. To change this setting, click on "Remove new document greeting" in your "Options" tab.

Chameleon Premiere 2.0 boasts up to 98% recognition accuracy, including transcription of contractions. Use your device's keyboard to edit the voice-recorded text if necessary.

Here are some basic voice command options: to insert a period, say "period"; to insert a comma, say "comma"; to go to a new paragraph, say "paragraph." (If you need to spell the words "period," "comma," or "paragraph," type them manually or turn off the punctuation and formatting command setting in your "Tools" tab.)

For more punctuation commands and other instructions, refer to your manual or click on the "Help" tab in the top right corner.

Okay here we go. This is going to be good. Think. Okay what's a good story what's a good story brainstorming will delete later. Okay so my main person is a man he needs a mission or a barrier keeping him from something. There should be a woman he likes maybe a man but I couldn't write that authentically. He likes a woman a woman leaves him he leaves a woman. No maybe he's alone. Yes he's alone he's a strong quiet type he lives on a ranch no in an apartment. He lives in a city a big one in downtown. He is around fifty he lost the love of his life a while ago and now he works at a hospital a homeless shelter a library maybe a restaurant a bartender no not a bartender that's too much like the movie we just saw. He is a cop and he is nice but mean when he has to be. He's in a small town actually a great plains state like a Nebraska or a western mountain state maybe like a Utah or a Montana. Okay okay keep these notes here we go a not yet titled novel by guy Nielson.

Darius Hendricks left the bar after it closed. He could have stayed longer because he knew the bartender, and was well respected and liked by everyone in the town of Montana city, but he had a feeling tomorrow was going to be a long day, and so he left the bar at two and he walked down the road because he was a good cop and there is no way he was going to go drunk driving. He had seen so much tragedy in his life, and he knew well the grim image of a car wrapped around a tree with the driver dead with his head bashed through the windshield. He thought to himself no way, and he slipped his keys into his pocket and started the long late night walk on the dusty road. As he was walking down the dusty road in his brown leather cowboy boots and denim jean jacket and cowboy hat, he got to thinking about his wife who died of an unsolved murder fifteen years ago and daddy sorry to bug you I can't sleep I had a bad dream oh no sweetie I'm sorry come here do you need some water you're safe in this house you know that you're always safe in this house I know but I had a bad dream about that bad guy with the mask in that space cat movie and he came into my room and he said give me your money and I said I don't have any money but I really had a dollar I was hiding and if it was a homeless person I would have given it to him to give him food but it was a bad guy and so he would have bought a sword or like you know a bad guy weapon honey it's okay it's okay I'll get you some water and tuck you in mommy put water by my bed already I just got scared and was going to crawl in your and mommy's bed but saw the light on over here okay sweetheart you're okay let me tuck you in what are you doing I'm writing a story can I read it you can when you're a little older I wrote a story for homework can I read it to you it's in my backpack I'm going to grab it okay honey then it's back to bed okay all right oh man this thing's been typing this out oh well will delete later okay here it is look at the picture I drew first see the picture of the girl dancing yeah it's great do you like it yeah nice work okay and here's the story that goes with it I used six vocabulary words but we only needed four but I just wanted to use six can I read it to you now sure of course once there was a girl named Tina and she was outside listening to extravagant music she had ballet music on and her dog was in the house observing out the window she loves to dance because she likes to move her feet and she is majestic when she was dancing her mom called her inside to go to bed and when she was asleep she had a bizarre dream of her dancing outside in the grass with giant ladybugs but then in the morning it was time for school after school she went in her backyard and did a jump and also scampered and then she was doing a dance for her family and they discovered that they loved her dance great job sweetheart I loved it that's really good I think that's really good thanks daddy and you have such neat handwriting look how small you're making your letters now can you tuck me in now I'm tired again of course kiddo will you tell me the story you're writing I'll tell you a different one will you lay down with me and say a new story and you can finish this book tomorrow and I'll write a new book tomorrow too okay okay

9

FEBRUARY HAD BEEN NICE, mostly in the 60s and 70s. And March was bearable, mostly in the 80s, but it had a few days break 90 to remind us of the hellish summer awaiting us all. And then April came and so did the regular heat. I hear that April is a pleasant spring month in most places, but it's not usually here. Usually, April brings the summer in the inland cities, and by April I didn't interact with Ronnie much. He was healed up and riding his bike all over town. I'd see him on the thing, around the bridge but also in downtown and other places in Riverside and Jurupa, and I'd think to myself, Was I always passing this guy? Was this guy always around before I'd hit him and I just didn't notice him? And I concluded that, Yeah, that must be the case, because now I saw that guy everywhere, even after he stopped calling.

And one night Ronnie called my phone when Ashley and I were on a date. It was a Friday night. We usually had dates on Friday and Saturday nights on account of her teaching Monday through Friday. Me? I'd have been up for a date any night because I don't have to do anything to get ready for work. But I can tell she's a good teacher. She's up reading things and working on lessons and writing notes on her students' essays and poems. She's a carer. She cares. And that meant no dates for me Sunday through Thursday night.

So Ronnie called in April when I was on a date with Ashley, and my phone was on vibrate and I let it go to voicemail. It went off a few times during dinner, then during the movie, and then I took Ashley home and went up to her place and we kissed for a while and kept chatting, and she decided not to make it a couch night. Maybe tomorrow night could be a couch night, she'd said. Maybe tomorrow night could finally be an I'm-in-your-bed-snuggling-up-with-you night, I was thinking. And then when I got in my car I finally listened to the voicemails—there were eleven of them—and Ronnie was freaking out and screaming but I couldn't make any sense of his ramblings.

I parked near the river bottom and got out of my car. I was uneasy being there at night. Over by the bridge there were streetlamps on, but I was walking away from that light and there was nothing but dark and gray in the direction of Ronnie's camp. No stars were visible either. But there was a good portion of the moon out. Luckily my cell phone had a good flashlight, so I turned that on and made my way down the slope to see if I could find Ronnie. The branches of small trees and shrubs brushed past me as I stepped ahead lightly. Some of the weeds were still tall and green, but most were starting to brown. The already-dead ones crunched under my feet, and foxtails were sticking to my pants and socks and biting at my ankles. In a few months, most of the weeds and brush away from the stream would be dead. Two-, three-, four-foot tall weed clusters all brown, tan, and white, all dead and needing clearing so they don't catch fire.

I got closer to where I thought Ronnie's tent was, but I couldn't locate it in the dark. My cell light was strong but it just lit up what was in front of me. I was walking so slowly that it felt like I had gone some great distance, but really I hadn't traveled that far and thought I should have seen his tent by now. I pointed the light at my feet, pointed it in front of me. Weeds and weeds, some shrubs, dirt, dirt, and more dirt, sporadic trees. I was about to give up when I heard a grunting sound. Grunting and squealing. I remembered Ronnie complaining about the loud lesbians in a nearby tent, and I couldn't help but laugh a little. I crept closer to the sound, just to help me get my bearings because I knew where the surrounding tents were in relation to his. I stalked closer. I turned off my light and moved by ear. The grunting and squealing got louder, and out of nowhere Ronnie's tent appeared, like an apparition or something, just popping out when I ducked under some small branches. The sound was coming from Ronnie's tent. His tent was dark on the inside and the outside. The burnt orange was gray in this light. Everything was cloaked in gray. His stuff was scattered around, his crates, the pop-up chair I'd gotten him. Henry was gone, or at least wandering around off-leash. His rope lay flat and curled on the dirt. I crouched down. I hoped that if Henry came across me he would remember my scent. I picked up a stone just in case.

I whispered, "Ronnie, Ronnie, is everything all right?" No one responded, but the grunting stopped. I whispered, "Ronnie, you called me. Is everything okay?" There was a stirring in the tent, some movement, but no one said anything. I crept closer, around to the opening. The main entrance flap was unzipped. Inside the opening it was dark. I whispered again, "Ronnie, you in there?" I thought, What the hell am I doing? Before the noises stopped, it sounded like Ronnie was in there pleasuring some homeless chick. I didn't need to see that. I didn't need to be interrupting that. But he was the one who'd called and screamed and screamed on my voicemails. I stalked to the entrance, hunched, nervous. I turned my cell's flashlight back on. The outside of the tent was burnt orange again. I directed the light into the opening. I couldn't see anything yet. "Ronnie," I said. "Ronnie." I stuck my head into the tent and had the light in front of me. To the right, backed against a tent side, a boar was staring at me. He was standing over Henry's body. Henry was dead, lying on his side, and his stomach was split open and the boar had been devouring him. I kept still. The light filled the tent because I didn't move my arms. I just knelt there. Still. My shoulders and head and arms were inside the musty tent while the rest of me stayed behind in the cool outside. Henry's tan hair was soaked red. His eyes were gone, eaten by the boar, his mouth was cracked open, and his tongue was gone too. There was still a lot of softness in the belly. A lot of soft red parts exposed. The boar had more work to do. I backed up slowly, keeping the light on the boar. It stayed. The light reflected in its eyes. Its tusks were red-soaked. I backed up until I could stand in the outside air. The boar stayed in the tent, and as I crept away, the grunting and squealing continued. It would continue until there were no good parts left. A lone male eating. The thing was at least twice the size of Henry. When I got to my car, I couldn't reach for my keys right away because I had the cell in one hand and the rock in the other. I dropped the rock. It thudded, and then my right hand and arm throbbed because I'd been clenching that thing so tightly. When I'd grabbed it, I was relieved that I'd found some sort of weapon, but I didn't process just how heavy it was. I had to rub my hand and arm for a minute before I could unlock my door.

Driving home, I wondered if there were a lot of boars living up and down the mostly-dry riverbed, or if that one was some anomaly. I wondered too what else that thing had been feeding on when Ronnie had heard its grunting in other nights.

That night, a dream. A mixture of memory and fabrication:

I walked down to the river bottom after a heavy rain. I was a boy. Maybe seven. Maybe eight. My best friend had spent the night. Mom told us to brush our teeth, so we did. Mom told us to go pee, so we stood side-by-side and peed into the same bowl, watching each other's streams, pretending they were light sabers, which made us both good guys since our pee streams were a yellow color closer to Luke's green saber than Darth Vader's red one. Then we moved on from *Return of the Jedi* and made jokes about not crossing the streams—we'd watched *Ghostbusters* second that night and giggled uncontrollably when Spengler said not to cross the proton streams while blasting a ghost. Of course we let our streams cross, our pee colliding midair, causing droplets to splash out, hitting the edge of the bowl, the floor, our bare feet. Then we were done and shook out the last drops and washed our hands and said our goodnights and fell asleep.

But I'd had a lot of grape soda, so I got up to pee again. Then I was awake and restless and thought about the things I might do. Mom was asleep on the couch, the TV's blue glow making her face like some alien or ghost. A commercial was on, something about preserving fruit in vacuum-tight storage bags. I put on my slippers and my bathrobe. I slipped out the back door, opening it and shutting it like a thief.

I climbed over our four-foot tall chain link fence and strolled down the sidewalk like everything was normal. I pictured myself running into passersby and saying things like, Good evening, Madam. And, Wonderful night for a stroll, is it not, my good man? But no one was out. I headed to the river bottom out of instinct. It was four blocks away. I'd play there during the day, keeping clear from the homeless people's tents, not touching needles in the sandy floor, beer bottles, used condoms. Only once before had I gone there at night. I'd made it to the edge, where the shrubs angle down to the mostly dried-up river bottom, and then I heard a howl or a hoot and darted home.

The sidewalk was wet. Had it really been raining? Yes. Yes, I was pretty sure at one point during the second movie Mom had passed the bowl of popcorn and said, "Hear all that rain, boys? It's really pouring." But I was focused on the woman with glasses with the interesting voice and wondering what it would be like to be married to her and have her sing to me in bed and hold me before and after we'd had sex. But yes, it had been raining, and when I got to the river bottom I saw that it had really poured because even from a distance and even in the gray light the stream that was now a river was rushing with a strength I'd never seen. I wasn't afraid this time. I was curious. And I slid down the embankment in my slippers and robe the same way I did during the day in my jeans. I was maybe thirty feet from the water. I crept closer. There was a camp of homeless people's tents across the river and down a way, but none where I was. The tents were dark and quiet, and I didn't hear any coyotes or owls either. I heard water, and when I got close to the edge, there was a big hole in the ground, right before the flowing stream. A hole that was a perfect circle, maybe three feet across. I knew a boy could get stuck in a hole like that, slip in like a pencil, arms pinned at his sides, then drown, or stay trapped until a buzzard ate his face. But

I looked down into the hole anyway. It was halfway full of water, and there was something floating in it. I poked the floating something with a stick. It moved. I couldn't tell what it was. I poked it again, and it uncurled itself, and it squealed, and it looked at me, and I saw a baby boar on top of a turtle.

I wanted to rescue this boar and turtle, these brave survivors of an unexpected downpour. I set my slippers to the side and climbed barefoot down into the hole. I thought, Careful. Careful. And I gripped the sides with my feet and legs like a compass, like an "A," half underwater, and I held the wall with one hand while another scooped the turtle into the crook of my arm with the baby boar still on top. I inched upward, my legs underwater, my chest and arms above water. It was a slow process. The turtle was pressed tight against my arm and chest. The baby boar was still. Perhaps scared. I concentrated on the wall, on my climbing, just sensing the boar in my peripheral. But then I turned my face to the boar. It lunged at an eye. I swung my face back toward the wall, and the boar missed my eye but got my ear. The boar bit down. It chewed my lobe. It worked on it quickly, and I felt little pieces of it leave me, and I felt blood or water slide down my neck, and I felt a screaming pain and a throbbing but I stayed silent and ground my teeth instead and focused on climbing, and I thought about tilting the turtle so that the boar would slide off and drown in the hole. I thought about saving the turtle and letting the boar suffer and drown. But I just kept climbing up and up, slowly so that I did not fall, and the baby boar took pieces of my ear while I gnashed my teeth, and then I made it out, and the boar jumped off the turtle and ran into the shrubs.

I fell on my back. And now I screamed. Now I cried, but I didn't touch my ear, and I stared at the sky for a minute while I caught my breath, the gray shapeless expanse sliding above like the stream beneath it. Then I sat up to see my turtle. I cradled the shell in my arms and rocked it. Its head and legs and tail were all tucked inside. I tried to coax its head out. I didn't know how. I reached two fingers and a thumb in and pulled on some skin. I brought its head out, its neck stretching, but its eyes were gone, eaten out by the baby boar, and its face was shredded, and the line that formed his mouth had little chunks taken out above it and below it. The area that would be lips. But turtles don't have lips really. Just a line. Or was this a tortoise? What it was was a shell with a neck and a sad stump of a head, a head and neck like a man's closed fist on a baby's arm. The turtle's sad head was moving around, searching the air, no eyes, no personality, just two nose holes and some divots where the boar had a chance to chew.

I felt bad for this turtle. What's a turtle's life without eyes? What chance did that thing have? I would have drowned it in the hole, but didn't turtles breathe underwater? Not all, or any, I guess, but I meant: didn't they hold their breaths a super long time? I stopped wondering that and I squeezed its neck before he could tuck his head back in and I grabbed a stick and I pierced him where I thought his brain was.

On the walk home, I had the turtle tucked into my bathrobe. I didn't want any late-night strollers to see me and think I was weird. I'd forgotten about my ear and the blood that was probably smeared on the left side of my head. The world was quiet, and I wondered if maybe I'd lost some of my hearing. Probably not. The sidewalk was still wet, and the concrete was cold on my feet. Damn, I thought. I'd forgotten my slippers. I could get them tomorrow. I hopped back into my yard, and I hid my dead turtle under a bush. I wanted to show it to my friend in the morning. Plus, I thought I'd like to scoop out the dead body and keep the shell in my room, if that kind of thing could be done. Backing away from the bush, I thought maybe I should take the turtle inside and start a bath for us. I could clean him up at least. But I wasn't allowed to start my own bath yet, and I didn't want to wake Mom. I left the turtle where he was and slipped back inside.

Mom was off the couch. I went to her room and kissed her cheek while she slept. A droplet of my ear blood fell on her cheek, and I left it there. I went into my bathroom. In the mirror I looked like me. I thought I wouldn't. I was hoping for something monstrous. But it was just me. I took a wet washcloth to my ear. I cringed. The voice I remembered to be my dad's said, That's a good boy. No whining. I didn't whine. I cleaned my ear. But it wouldn't stop bleeding. I'd wipe it clean. Then it would bleed again. I was missing some bits of lobe. I took a dry washcloth, pressed it to my ear, then wrapped some medical tape around my head to keep it in place. I slipped my robe off. I thought I saw some pecs developing. I went into my room and climbed into the top bunk, careful not to step on my friend below. In bed I stared at the ceiling, trying to hear some night bird or wild animal, but there was nothing.

VII

A Boy and His Mother

ONCE A BOY GOT on all fours and screamed at his mother, "Look. I'm a bear."

The mother said, "There are no bears in these parts."

The boy shuffled his four legs, strutted in a circle, licked a front paw, then said, "Look. I'm a mountain lion."

"Oh," said the mother, "oh, I'm sorry to lose you, but you'd better go live in the wilderness now. I can't have a mountain lion ruining my carpet."

The mountain lion said, "You've been a good mother, so I won't eat you now, but you'd do well to avoid strolling near the honeysuckle shrubs down by those gangly rosewoods. That area's going to be my lair."

The mother beamed at how well her mountain lion knew his terrain. She opened the sliding glass door and let the budding lion outside. The mother was sadder now than when her husband curled up and turned into a boulder. She'd set the boulder in the front garden as a lovely accent, but somewhere along the way someone stole it, probably in a wheelbarrow, probably two or three bodies to do the job since no one else on the earth had the strength she did to lift and plant that boulder.

Past the backyard, the mountain lion curled beneath a honeysuckle and began to groom himself. He felt a tug in his brain, a voice saying, Hey, you were only supposed to live here for playtime. But the mountain lion roared that playtime was over and this was home now and then devoured what was left of the delicate voice.

10

BACK WHEN WE HAD our first date, Ashley asked me if I believed in God. I didn't hesitate. I answered yes right away. Because I do. I wasn't trying to answer the right way for her or anything. I do believe in God. Wholeheartedly. I was never good at articulating why. Just something inside. Just a presence I suppose. But Ashley didn't ask me to articulate because by that point in the dinner I'd found out she taught at a Christian college, so I knew she was on board with that. I told her I grew up Catholic before my dad left us, and then my mom took us to the Presbyterian church on and off. It wasn't upbringing, though, that made me believe in God. And I wouldn't call myself a Christian, just someone who believes in God.

And I was glad she left the discussion there because I was interested in her and I didn't want to come off looking like some heathen to her or something. But I could tell I didn't. And then we talked about our families and where we grew up and ran through the regular first-date litany. She went to a good small college in Ohio near where she grew up, double-majoring in English and psychology, and then she did grad programs in Michigan and Illinois, still not venturing too far from home, getting what she called an MFA in writing poetry and then a PhD in American lit. I said I didn't know there were degree programs for learning how to write poems, and she laughed and sipped her wine and said that you need to know how to write poems already before getting into a program like that. They just made you better. When she asked me if I went to college and I told her that I did and that I was an English major, too, with a second major in philosophy before I dropped it for a variety of reasons, she looked at me real unsure for a moment, had a face with a crinkled brow like, Is he being serious or joking? I really do not know and it could go either way.

I was serious. I said, "Yeah, no, I really was. Since I grew up out here I just attended RCC for two years after high school and then transferred to Cal State San Bernardino for a few more. I didn't know how much I liked to read until I got to college, so the English major came out of nowhere but I thought it would give me good options for my future. And what I loved about philosophy was ethics, thinking about these little stories, these hypothetical situations people might be in, as individuals and groups, and then debating what is the right thing to do. You know, given this unique circumstance, what is the right thing for this individual or for this group to decide. I finished a few years ago and just kept working at the café because I don't need much to live on. I'll find a better job one day I'm sure. But for now I don't mind my life, I guess. And maybe that's the value of a college degree these days, huh. Maybe I'm destined to just make sandwiches."

"I think you just keep doing what you want to do," she said. "There's nothing wrong with that. There's nothing wrong with your job. It's a good job. You'll find your way into something else if that's what you want. Otherwise, yeah, just keep making those sandwiches and helping damsels in distress choose the right avocados."

I was going to say something cheesy about not wanting to help anyone else out with their fruit and vegetable needs or wanting to be her vegetable man or something stupid like that, and I was glad I didn't try to be clever or charming and risk coming across as desperate, and I made a good decision because I just said, "Yeah, thanks for that."

Her parents were still together and her siblings lived scattered throughout the Midwest, none of them more than a day's drive from her folks' place. I told her I'd never been, said I'd seen snow only once, as a kid, when my dad took me up to Big Bear one winter for a day of sledding. She couldn't believe it. She said she didn't know how people dealt with six months of heat out here. I said you don't think about it when it's all you know. But that wasn't really true. I hated the heat even though I was used to it.

When that first date ended I knew I wanted to see her again. I didn't know if she'd be up for it, but I knew I'd ask. When I made it home, I couldn't sleep. I read for a while, got up and walked around my apartment, read some more, got restless again and walked around my living room and then walked myself out of my door and down the stairs and got in my car and drove drove drove.

I headed south. And I then I headed west. I ended up in La Jolla, a ritzy beach town I'd go to sometimes in high school. I had this wealthy friend in Riverside whose family moved down there for his dad's work. He switched high schools of course, and because he didn't know people right away he would invite me down to the weekend parties, and I'd show up and drink with him and joke around with the prep boys he was hanging out with, but I never wanted to stay down there at his new house, and I'd make like I was just going to hit the road and go back north, but I wasn't stupid enough to drive a long distance after I'd been drinking, so I'd drive the few blocks to the coast and park, and I found this little beach you had to get to by going down a long staircase, and it was tucked in around some short cliffs, and I would pull a blanket out of my car and go down and pass out on the beach. Every time I'd go down to see him at some party, I'd look forward to it because I always slept at that little beach, and no one ever bothered me. I just laid my blanket out on a piece of sand near the rock wall so no one would spot me from above, and I'd stare at the sky, and I'd fall asleep to the waves and the cold salt air, and when the sun crept out, I'd get up quickly, hop in my car, and drive the hour and a half home, wondering if my mom would know or care that I'd been out all night.

So that was where I drove when I couldn't sleep after my first date with Ashley. And I felt guided there, like that was where I needed to go. And I hadn't slept out there on that beach for over ten years, and I hadn't thought about those days much, but for whatever reason my head and body took me there, and I parked where I'd remembered the right staircase being. And there were bigger houses than I'd remembered and lots of new construction going on, people trying to cram in as many ocean views as possible. But I didn't park in the right place, or maybe I did but the secluded beach from my past had changed. There were fewer boulders around and more sand. You couldn't really hide as easily if you wanted to sleep down there. And there were more lights. More lights lining the pathway above.

I didn't think I'd be able to sleep down there with all the light and openness, but I was amped from my date with Ashley anyway. And I said aloud, because it just occurred to me then, "Why the hell didn't I ever swim down here?" And I stripped down to my boxers and tucked my clothes and shoes behind some rocks, and then I took off my boxers too because, why the hell not, and I ran out into the breaking waves all intense like I was in some ironman competition, and the sand was real gravelly there, not smooth at all, rough and thick, and the water was freezing, but I charged forward until I was waist deep, then dove forward into a wave as it was about to break. I popped up out the other side and my body shuddered in the cold, kind of shocked and vulnerable feeling, like the fact that I was alive and a living thing was made apparent in some new way, and I did the crawl for a few paces and got out into the deep. I wasn't a graceful swimmer, but I could tread water for a long time.

I stayed out there treading water for an hour or two, maybe more. Every once in a while I swam a few strokes back toward the shore so the tide didn't carry me out. I talked to God out there. I talk to God more often than I admit to most folks. Is Ashley the girl for me? I asked Him. I can't tell you that yet, He said, but you'll find out soon enough. I think I want it to be her, I said. I know I do, I mean, but only if it's your will, I said. And He said, I'll make my will clear enough. You'll have clarity for that at least pretty soon, He said. And I gave Him thanks for that. And I treaded and bobbed and treaded and sometimes swam a few strokes to shore. And we talked again about older matters like my dad's leaving and how I'm not responsible for anyone's thoughts but my own and how my thoughts are generally pleasing to Him and when they're occasionally not they're not all that weird or anything because I am after all a human being all crammed with desires of various kinds and fears and insecurities and the like.

Soon enough my limbs were hard as bone and there was no softness to me, my skin tight at the ribs, shriveled from the cold. I swam clumsily to the shore, and I was grateful when the waves propelled me forward because I really thought then that if I sank to the bottom I might have been too tired not to drown. I was pushed to the sand and then I crawled out of the water's lick and flipped myself over. I slept there for an hour or two or three, my limbs outstretched, my nakedness on display for the moon and stars and probably no one else. Before I fell asleep, my cold body urged me to get to the warm car. But tiredness beat out comfort. So I slept in the wet sand and shivered until the cold went away and all was silent. When I woke, it was still dark. I brushed off what sand I could and found where I'd stashed my clothes and keys. It stayed night for the whole drive home.

VIII

Once a Dozen Strangers

ONCE A DOZEN STRANGERS explored a cave system in western Kentucky. They'd met online in a chatroom for twenty-first-century explorers who "go off the beaten path!" who "despise the velvet ropes!" that "money-making organizations!" "slap around nature!" "corralling in tourists!" with their "big cameras!" and "once-a-year boots!"

The dozen strangers met in a parking lot. They shook hands. They admired each other's gear. Then they walked, walked, walked until there were no cars or roads or other people, and they found an entry into the underworld of Kentucky, and they beamed, and they awed, and they knew their terms, saying things like "pit" and "shaft" and "dome" and "bedding plane" and "dead cave"—"wait, no—*live cave!* because hear that water?" and "stalactites" and "cave coral" and "gypsum flower" and "rockmilk" and "dark zone," occasionally settling on the necessary but less exciting terms like "room" and "mouth" and "passage." And they all had good flashlights to point "There!" and "Right there!" And then eleven of the twelve strangers got trapped in a dead pit when the last one couldn't quite squeeze his way in to join the others. He was really stuck. And because a dead pit doesn't have passages extending past the entry, which is why it's called a dead pit, of course, they needed to get the guy unstuck for them to slip out and keep going.

What happened was this: eleven of them squeezed into the space after one of them first made the discovery, saying, "Nice, you've got to check this out." And one by one they maneuvered through the narrow opening to check it out, following each other down a gentle slope into the pit, but the last guy was a bit bigger than the others. He wasn't overweight. Just a bit bigger. And he really wanted to get inside with the other eleven once they were in, so he tossed his backpack through the slit, and he breathed in and tried to force himself through sideways, but he ended up with one arm in and one out, and one leg in and one out, and his face was sideways, stuck between the rocks, looking down the passageway they'd just come from, so that the eleven already in the pit were staring at half his body and the back of his head, shouting, "Slide out" and "You idiot" and "Jerk back," and he'd responded, "I can't" and "I'm not" and "I can't," so then the eleven huddled together and discussed the matter.

Without asking permission, one of them violently yanked on the stuck guy's arm and then his leg, tugging like a wild man. But he didn't budge. Then three of them rammed him repeatedly. But he didn't budge. Some of them screamed for help along with the stuck one, yelling, yelling, until their voices gave out. And for a long while various members of the eleven pushed and pulled, but nothing happened. Some ridiculed him, calling him an "Imposter" and a "Disgrace," and a few cursed at him, saying he was a "Fat fuck," and some just sat weeping, watching tears slap the rock floor by flashlight. Eventually they all agreed there was no budging him. His body plugged the passageway like it had been shaped for this very purpose, to fuse with the cool, hard opening.

Then the stuck one said, "Sorry. I'm really very sorry. I just wanted to see in there, too." And one said, "I understand. It is so beautiful in here." And another echoed, "Yes, so beautiful in here."

And the eleven conferenced again, taking inventory of their supplies. And they all had very fine knives, and they found the stuck one's very fine knife, too. Some were long, some short. Some had standard straight back blades, others a hawkbill or a drop point. One even had a gut hook. And another had a needle point. The twelve knives were new, gleaming under their flashlights. One had a striking rosewood handle, another an equally impressive beechwood.

The idea floated out from a few of them, then whispered around their circle: "We could kill him, might be the only way to get ourselves out."

They asked the stuck man about this possibility. "If pushing you out won't work, and it seems like it won't, do you mind if we kill you real quick, then carve our way through you?"

And the stuck man said, "Yes, I do mind. Which is to say, No. Don't kill me."

And the eleven conferenced again, and then they said to him, "We'd really like your permission to do this. We'd feel better about all of this if you'd say something like, 'Sure, I guess I'm to blame here and I'm okay with you killing me so you can save yourselves.'"

But the stuck man said, "I'm not okay with that. I don't want you doing that." And then he said, "I think we should wait for help. Let's try waiting for help."

Time passed. And again the eleven pushed and they pulled, and the stuck man wouldn't budge. They said to him, "The air is not so great in here anymore." They said to him, "We'd really like it if you'd tell us that you're okay with us killing you, real fast remember, and then cutting ourselves free." They said, "I think now's the time for you to give us the green light on that so we can go on living."

But the stuck man said, "Keep holding out a little longer, you guys. You're doing great. I can feel it. I can feel help is on the way." And he yelled, "Help! Help!" for a while longer since he wanted to be able to contribute something. And since his face pointed toward the passage they'd come in through, he had plenty of oxygen and felt the smallest breeze now and then, the damp air offering little licks on his chin, nose, and forehead while the rock walls held his chest and back and crotch and cheeks.

The next day the eleven suffocated, and the stuck man had slept okay for being gripped upright in rock. When he woke, he called to them, and he figured they had run out of oxygen when no one responded. And he felt terrible. Truly terrible. He stayed stuck for three more days, and when he woke on the fourth morning he fell out of the rock's clutches and smacked the floor. He couldn't look back into the pit. Instead, he crawled slowly toward the earth's opening, winding this way, then that way, and eventually he pushed himself through the earth's slit like a mouse or a badger leaving its burrow for a bit of sustenance.

Outside, he crawled a while longer until he had the strength to stand and then walk, and he slowly made it back to his car. He pulled his keys from his pocket, and he opened his trunk, where he kept a safety-supply kit complete with emergency drinking water, and he gulped, not too fast, but still he gulped, gulped, gulped in a smooth, measured way, and after his stomach contained two twelve-ounce bottles of mountain water, he closed the trunk and opened his door, and the eleven other cars were still there, but he didn't focus on them. He didn't want their details imprinted in his memory. They were only eleven blurred rectangles and ovals in his peripheries, all some shade of silver or tan. And then he focused on the road when the parking lot was behind him, and he headed home, thinking he should say something aloud, thinking it would be a good thing to talk about all of this if only to himself. And after he was miles down the road, after he was on the right path home, his mouth opened and he said, "Oh my." And he tried for something else, but all he could do was sigh and shake his head and say, "Oh my. Oh my."

11

WHEN I WAS A LITTLE kid, my great aunt shared my room. She was childless, so Mom claimed her. She slept in the bottom bunk. I was in the top. How long was she there for? I don't know. Six weeks? Six months? It wasn't a full year. Some of second grade and some of summer.

She would wake up every night, stand up, and not know where she was. She would stare at me for a while. She was a tall, thin woman. Even in her eighties, she stood tall, no slouching, no humpback for her. She'd wake and stand and stare at my face, our heads right by each other.

In the beginning, I'd open my eyes and there she'd be, inches away, trying to figure out who I was and where she was. She'd call me Tommy, my cousin's name, or she'd grunt or even shriek, and I'd say, "Calm down, Aunt Liesel. It's me, Joe. You're in my room." Sometimes she'd settle down and go back to bed. Most of the time she'd do something else: go into the kitchen and start throwing out our food until Mom stopped her, try to turn on the TV and then scream in frustration until she'd break dishes, lamps, her own ceramic figurines until Mom stopped her.

Eventually I learned to keep my eyes closed. I'd hear wheezing, then smell her sour breath, feel hot spittle on my nose, cheeks, eyelids. Still I'd keep my eyes closed tight, hoping she'd leave my room, cursing her for not having at least one child to burden. Every once in a while, she'd kiss my cheek and crawl back into the bunk below. Sometimes she'd try to climb into my bed, but she'd get stuck on the bottom bar. Sometimes she'd stand so close her nose would brush against my cheek. A couple of times she kissed my nose but then opened her mouth and left her lips there, circling my nose, wet and clumsy like a fish chomping on a bottle. Still I'd keep my eyes shut, riding it out until she'd leave the room or go back to bed.

During the day she'd keep to my room, taking over my desk, using up my good markers with nonsense notes. Mom would bring her food, set plates down on the desk and creep backwards to the door. Sometimes Aunt Liesel would eat. Sometimes she'd emerge in the hallway, a burger in hand, a burrito in hand, and she'd hurl the food at Mom, shouting, "Goddamnit. What goddamn shit is this," and rage back to my room and slam my door. And Mom would look at me and say, "Remember what she was like before this. Just cling to those memories. Okay?" And I'd say, "Okay." But I didn't have those memories.

Sometimes she'd ask us to leave her house. "Why are you still here?" she'd say. "Can't you see Christmas is over?"

She'd wander the neighborhood, and we'd drive around slowly until we found her. We'd pull over and scoop her up, say things like, "There you are. It's macaroni-and-cheese night, Aunt Liesel. Come on home."

One night she did manage to climb my ladder and get into my bunk with me. I heard her creaking up the ladder, hoping she'd not be able to take each next step. But she made it up somehow. And she positioned herself next to me. And we were spooning, her on the outside. And I let her have that. She curved to me, poking me with her ribs. And she breathed onto my neck, and she kissed the back of my head, and I let her have that. I stayed quiet. I pretended I was being watched over by an angel who needed me to be still to give her this moment. But then she climbed over me, and she repositioned herself so that our stomachs were facing. We would have been hugging except I kept my arms pulled to my chest, kept them there in the prayer pose they'd been in, my fingers clasped. The tips of our noses touched, and then she inched herself up toward my pillow. My nose grazed her neck as she moved. Then my nose grazed her robe. And still I kept my eyes closed tight. And her hands must have opened her robe because the fabric brushed my cheek but then was replaced with her skin pushing against me, and a cold hand took hold of my lips, squeezing them hard so that my lips puckered, and she was forcing something into my lips, back and forth, but I clenched my teeth. My jaw wasn't going to budge. But she worked on my mouth with her hand, trying to break through my teeth, a boney finger tapping, tapping, tapping. And something was sliding in and out of my lips but getting no further. And she whispered, "Baby needs the nipple." And she hummed a tune I didn't know. And her fingers gripped my lips so tight they were becoming numb, and she kept forcing her nipple between my puckered lips, and I felt her sliding in and out until I was finally numb to the feeling.

I didn't move. I'm not sure why. Other than feeling like I'd already decided I was pretending to be asleep and needed to stick with it. And I didn't want her to get in trouble. I just wanted her gone. Mom found us sleeping like that in the morning. I woke when Mom gently said to her, "Come on down, dear. Your bed's down here." And she tucked her in, then kissed me on the cheek and called me her sweet boy.

IX

[The Cora Fragment]

... AND THEN WHEN SHE was ten her parents discovered the word trichotillomania, and they kissed the little wounds on her head and told her, "You're our beautiful girl, okay?" and they sat in the breakfast nook in the morning glow and told her, "It's called TTM, and we are here for you, and we love you," and they put band-aids on her fingertips to deter the pinching, but when her parents were distracted by the wonders around them—her dad enraptured by the yellow leaves giving up their grip, loosening from their limbs just like that, so delicately—her mom staring intently at the word *through* in the headline of her newspaper, whispering to the word, "What's your story with all those letters?"—in moments such as these, she would pinch a single strand and tug and sometimes she could dislodge the root and sometimes the strand would slide through her fingers while wrapped in their band-aids, but even those tugs felt better than nothing, and when she did succeed in plucking strands with her parents close by, she'd slip the stems in her mouth, tucking them in a cheek where her tongue could glide over the bits of skin stuck to the roots.

This pleasure excited her, and she did not yet feel guilt for her body, and she did not seek punishment for her body, even as it betrayed her time and again, her parents conducting their inspections, their fingers gliding along her scalp, parting strands to expose the circular patches of skin, like burnished pennies in their bright kitchen

light. Her parents wept. They said, "Cora, dear, dear Cora, we are doing this for you. We are doing this for you."

By age twelve, her parents had resorted to putting thick mittens
on her hands before bed, duct-taping them to the sleeves of a long-
sleeved shirt so as not to harm her soft wrists when they unbound
them in the morning.

Then it happened that on the day Cora turned thirteen, the holy
saint Guthmara moved into the little cottage next door, and we have
spoken of her life earlier and made clear the miracles she worked in
town in her youth and in the final earthly home she treated as a cell,
a refuge where she humiliated demons nightly, demons not once suc-
ceeding in their torments even as they pulled her from her cell and
took flight across the wilderness, across remote rivers, cutting her
body through thick brambles before depositing her miles away to
walk home in the ice-cold morning. And you have heard about her
many visitors during the day, travelers seeking her wisdom. But now
hear how Cora met her and learned from her before she departed this
world.

Cora and her mom were returning from a walk when the moving van arrived, and they stood and watched a young man carry in a
microwave, a sewing machine, two end tables, a twin bed and mattress,
a rectangular table, its disconnected legs, and thirteen mismatched
chairs. And then he dollied in two boxes of dishes and one box of
books. Cora's mom perked up at the tall books peeking out of the box,
and Guthmara emerged from nowhere and said, "Could you help me
unpack them?" And Cora's mom said, "Yes, please." And they went into
the cottage, and Guthmara asked them to line up the books against
the wall so they were handy, and mother and daughter said the books
were exquisite, and she said there were many more in years past, but
you can't take them with you, and you find that what you really need
in the end should be stored in your head if you have been allowed to
grow into wrinkles, and Cora smiled when Guthmara had said, "Grow
into wrinkles," and then Cora's mom finished lining up several beige
volumes with deckled edges, and she opened one and said, "You know
Jerome's Latin?"

So started the beginning of Cora's parents saying, "Okay," whenever Cora asked, "Can I go to Ms. Mara's house?" And how could they
say no? The girl was happier, stronger in body and brain, disciplining

herself to pinch and pull out only seven hair strands in each private session while the band-aids were on her fingers, and allowing only one session a week on Fridays (later it would be every other Friday while incorporating mild fasting, and later her parents would be so impressed with their scalp inspections that they stopped duct-taping her mittens to her wrists at night and even putting band-aids on her fingertips each morning), and the girl was taught that the quiver of her body was not a sin, and the girl was taught that she needed to decide when and how often to enjoy such pleasures once she had control of her urges.

In the beginning, when she was trying to master her urges, she would pull out a notecard from her pocket, reading aloud:

Benedicam Dominum in omni tempore;
semper laus eius in ore meo.
In Domino laudabitur anima mea;
audiant mansueti et laetentur.
Magnificate Dominum mecum,
et exaltemus nomen eius in id ipsum!
Exquisivi Dominum, et exaudivit me,
et ex omnibus tribulationibus meis eripuit me. (Et cetera)

And while Cora read the Latin from her notecard she simultaneously meditated on the English translation dancing through her mind because the saint had taught her well. And so she thought:

I'll speak well of the Lord in all seasons;
His praise will always be there in my mouth.
In the Lord my soul will be praised;
let the gentle ones hear and be cheered up.
Make the Lord splendid with me,
and let us lift up His name together!
I searched for the Lord, and he understood me,
and he snatched me from all my sufferings. (as well as the rest ...)

And eventually she did not need the notecards and whispered to herself in bed, at the breakfast table, in the shower:

Deus noster refugium et virtus,
adiutor in tribulationibus,
quae invenerunt nos nimis. (Et cetera)

Which unfolded in Cora's mind as:

God is our shelter and strength,
our supporter in sufferings,
which have found us so often. (and the rest . . .)

And while walking down the sidewalk or in the woods behind her
house, she'd sing:

Miserere mei, Deus; miserere mei,
quoniam in te confidit anima mea,
et in umbra alarum tuarum sperabo
donec transeat iniquitas. (Et cetera)

And those opening verses had a special folder in her mind, and she
would repeat them two, three, four times before finishing the rest of
the psalm, thinking again and again:

Feel pity for me, God. Feel pity for me,
because my soul depends on you,
and in the shadow of your wings I'll find hope
until this shamefulness passes. (and eventually the rest . . .)

And many others, and many others, because she learned that her mind
was a vault endlessly expanding despite its bone enclosure.

The last item of importance concerning Cora and Guthmara together is the miraculous vision they shared. Once on a Friday evening
after Cora had allowed herself to pluck seven strands from a patch of
skin near her right ear, she was sleeping happily when the vision came.
She traveled through the gray night, gliding through air, surveying the
ground sharply like an owl except she did not know what she was supposed to be looking for. She soared north through a dense forest until
she shot into a clearing, and there was a river with a mild current cutting through the field, and as she flew closer to it, she saw Guthmara's
body, smooth and tender, lying lifelessly. Cora hovered in the air, un-
able to control her direction, watching the rest unfold. The holy body
was stretched out, uncovered, on the hard winter's ground. The skin
gleamed. Her hands were folded on her abdomen. Her nipples were
relaxed despite the chill. Her eyes were open, golden instead of walnut,
looking up past where Cora floated. Her closed lips smiled. Her hair
was still white but her body more youthful.

Then a man came walking along the river and stopped at the
body. He didn't seem surprised to see her. Cora then understood that
this man was scheduled to meet her there. He wore a brown robe, and

she gathered that he was a monk and one of her former disciples. He wept profusely, so much so that his tears drenched her feet. Then he slowly washed her feet with those tears, and he performed a prayer for her burial though Cora could not understand the words, and then he sang, and she recognized it to be psalm-singing though, again, she could not make sense of the language. And Cora marveled at how this man beheld her body not as a thing to be prodded. He knelt beside her and lifted her hands to clasp his cheeks. He kissed her palms, then returned her hands to their folded position.

Then he surveyed the ground. He walked around the holy body. He settled on a low-lying spot past her head, and then his fingers attempted to break into the earth. He could not penetrate the cold ground. He grabbed a nearby branch and attempted to dig with it, but the stick broke in two with its first thrust. He stood up and seemed to think about his next step. And that is when an enormous lion emerged from the forest, peering at the man while striding toward him. The man removed his robe, quickly covered the holy body. He stood naked, genitals exposed, hands folded together and placed on top of his head in an act of submission. He awaited the massive creature. He yelled, "Ferocious beast, if you were sent here by God to entrust this sacred woman to the earth, begin your work. But if you were sent from someone else, devour me to satisfy your craving, but do not so much as sniff the holy body beside me unless you wish an angel of God to slice you lengthwise." The lion stopped where the man had attempted to dig. Its claws scraped the ground, breaking through with ease, removing clod after clod. In little time the lion's great forelegs produced a grave several feet deep and the exact length to fit the sacred body. Then the man and lion worked together to move her. He lifted her up at the shoulders, and the lion slid his head beneath her calves so that her feet alighted on its mane. Like this they walked the body to the grave and laid it inside, and the man did not retrieve his cloak, and the lion scooped dirt onto the body until all the displaced earth had been returned. And there was a rise in the earth, but the lion stomped on the mound until the soil was packed tightly and flattened so that no passerby would be alerted to the gem beneath. Then the lion returned to the woods, and the man walked along the river, naked and alone, in the same direction from where he came.

Cora awoke on Saturday while the morning was dark, and in her robe and slippers she walked over to Guthmara's house and found her sitting on the front porch, singing softly while sipping tea. There was an extra mug waiting for Cora. Cora sat and took the warm porcelain in her hands. Guthmara said, "You've seen the burial, so don't seek the body when you come here one day and can't find me." Cora said, "Okay." And Guthmara said, "It's easy to rejoice all the time when you remember that earthly pain is a speck beside the glory awaiting in heaven." And Cora smiled, and she kept smiling, and they sat until they finished their tea, and then Cora said, "Thank you," and went back home where her dad was in the kitchen making pancakes. Later that day then when Cora was . . .

12

THE MORNING AFTER I SAW the boar eating Henry, Ronnie called again, and I answered right away. It was around 6:00 a.m., and I hadn't slept well. He said, matter-of-factly, that Henry died and that he needed to get a new dog today. I asked him what happened, and he said, "Old age. Old age happened." Henry had died while sleeping in the tent. Ronnie was lying down reading a sci-fi novel—he likes to check those ones out from the library, he told me once—and while he was reading he eventually noticed Henry was dead. He didn't mention the boar. Just kept saying, "Old age." I guess the boar must have sniffed out the dead body when Ronnie was out of the tent. I felt better knowing that the boar didn't attack and kill the dog first. Unless Ronnie was lying about it for some reason. Unless Ronnie let the boar kill the dog so he could get away.

Ronnie said he called me, and I said I was out with my girl and forgot my phone. "You have a girl," he said. "All right, man. Way to go, man. I had a wife once, a mortgage once, all that. Hey, man. I need to get a new dog today, man."

I agreed to meet him at the dog park. He wanted me to drive to a shelter and pick out a dog for him, said they wouldn't give one to him, had to be someone else. "What about Ace?" I said. "Out of town," he said. "Why I called you last night. Ace is visiting his daughter in Utah, man." I didn't say that I'd dropped by that night. I kept waiting for him to bring up the boar or Henry's devoured carcass or the bloody mess in his tent, but he never did, so I never asked him about it. He said after he couldn't get a hold of me, he'd gone out at night wandering around in search of abandoned dogs in the river bed. He said the dog park in the early morning is another good place to find dogs. When people don't want to turn dogs into a shelter, when they're too lazy or they don't want to be caught on paper, they go to the dog park in the late night or early hours and toss their dog inside. No collar, no identification, just a dog in the fenced-in park. They know that when people show up to exercise their dogs in the morning, they'll call animal control to come get it. Sometimes though people just keep one they find. Some people, Ronnie said, will be like, "Shit, I've got two dogs. I'll take a third." Or, "I've got three dogs. I'll take a fourth." There's this one woman who parks at the base of Mt. Rubidoux at 5:00 a.m. every day, seven days a week, said Ronnie, and she parks her van there and hops out and hikes the backside of the mountain, the unpaved parts, and has eleven dogs in tow. Eleven dogs, mostly Shepherds, running around but staying near her. And then after an hour or so, they follow back into the van and hop in obediently, and then she's out of there before most people are out of their beds. She's out of there and only Ronnie and a handful of people in the world know the Shepherd lady exists.

I drove to the shelter with Ronnie. The animal shelter, not the human shelter, as he'd said. We went to the one on Van Buren in Jurupa Valley. The cheap one, he'd called it. The big one where you barely have to fill out any papers. They're dying to hand out dogs there so they don't have to kill them.

He'd given me a wish list of sorts. Henry was mostly Rhodesian Ridgeback and had something else in him too. Maybe some Lab and Pit. He said I probably wouldn't find a Rhodesian, but if I did, grab it. As long as it was a male that wasn't too old. He'd found Henry abandoned in the dog park one morning. Even saw the car skid away after some guy walked it into the park, removed its collar, shut the gate, and darted to his still-running car. Henry was somewhere around nine to twelve months old then, somewhere between the puppy and adult stage. The adolescent dogs got dropped off most often. Dogs past small-puppy cuteness. Dogs bursting with energy, destroying things. Dogs, Ronnie said, saying, Man, I want to go fuck things up. I'm a dog, man. Let's go destroy some shit. I'm like a teenager dog. What you'd expect from me, man?

So that was between ten and fifteen years ago, Ronnie said, when he'd found Henry. And now Ronnie's wish list consisted of: a male dog definitely; not under twelve months unless it's a real find, and then absolutely not under eight or nine months; preferably not over four years; we're aiming for two to four, but you can go up to five maybe six years old if need be; no, scratch that, stay at four and under; a Rhodesian if possible but probably not realistic; a Shepherd of some kind; a Lab of some kind; definitely not a pure Pit or a pure Rottweiler; but mixes okay, like a Lab with Pit or a Shepherd with Rott; a large-size dog; large does not mean Great Dane; that's extra-large; large does not mean some small forty-pound thing; large, said, Ronnie, means sixty to ninety pounds; and no Husky; you'll see a lot of Huskies in there because people like the idea of them but then can't handle them; they're almost too wild; they're definitely too stubborn.

To all that, I said, "Okay. I'll do my best." Ronnie stayed in the car, didn't want to be caught on the cameras he said were outside the building.

The shelter was real nice. The dog area was called like Puppy Paradise or something even though most of the dogs were all old. But everything was real clean. I was impressed. And they had two dogs to a kennel, a real large kennel, more like a room, that had its own area inside the air-conditioned building and then a doggy door to its own outside area. People could walk around the outside too and peer over into the various enclosures, like we were at the zoo or something. I walked along the inside hallway and looked at the typed-up descriptions on the outside before I really paid much attention to the actual dogs. I was looking for age and weight and sex, and then I would consider the breed. Eventually I found a Cattle Dog I liked. The girl who worked there said it was big for a Cattle Dog, that they're normally more like in the forty- to fifty- pound range, and this was a two-year-old male that was seventy pounds. He was mixed with a few things, she said, maybe some Lab, maybe some Pit. It can be hard to tell. When desire strikes, you never know who's going to hop over the fence. We get some crazy mixes in here, she said.

I took that one, the large Cattle Dog. Australian, the girl said, still has strong herding instincts. You might find him herding you. And we laughed at that, and I filled out the papers, put my address down, and they plugged my phone number into the microchip system. I was a little nervous about that, or felt a bit deceptive. And then as the girl congratulated me and this dog on our new life together, on our new *lifelong* journey together, she'd emphasized, I felt pretty guilty. Walking the dog out to the car, I rationalized that a life in the river bottom with Ronnie was better than being in the shelter and waiting to be put to death if no one takes you. But I was kidding myself, because this was a good-looking dog, and someone else would have taken him eventually. There were plenty of old ratty-looking dogs that would get put down, but this one, someone else would have snatched him up if I hadn't grabbed him for Ronnie.

Ronnie sat in the backseat with the dog on the drive back to his campsite, on the drive back to where mountain base and dog park and bridge and Riverside and Jurupa and Santa Ana River all stream together—all stream together in a mess of weeds and dirt and sparse trees and a little water.

Ronnie said he was going to spend some time bonding with the dog before he brought it into the dog park, said he wanted to train it a bit, have it listen, before he let it see other dogs and people. I asked if he was good on food and water, and he said he was. I didn't walk down to see him tie the new dog to

Henry's rope or see if Henry's carcass had been buried and the blood cleaned up.

X

A Boy and His Father

ONCE A BOY TRUDGED up a hill with a potted chrysanthemum. The pot was wider than he was, but his thin arms managed to encircle the clay, and he embraced that weight from home to hill somehow. When he reached the clearing at the top, he took his place at Table 7, just as his acceptance letter had directed him to do. He picked up a marker and two sticker nametags from the table and wrote *Joey* on one and *Chris* on the other. He stuck *Joey* on himself, careful not to block any part of the stegosaurus on his chest, and he stuck *Chris* on the pot just under the lip.

Then the director of the Silky Valley Father/Son Picnic and Potato Sack Race Extravaganza approached the boy and said, "Welcome, Joey! And welcome, Chris!" And the director turned his back to the plant and whispered to the boy, "Now is that your father there in that pot? Or is that your son? Because you look a little young to be a dad."

And the boy said, "This is my father's pot. I was thinking about bringing his shoes, on account of the race, but my father used this pot to grow many things, like Chris here, which he planted three years ago."

The director turned back to the plant, looked him over, then said to the boy, "Are you sure he's not your father? Observe how he's tilting toward you. That's genuine concern there. Such protection. Don't worry, sir! I'm just speaking to the boy! Nothing else! And look at the resemblance. I see it now, how the swoop of your cheeks is the same as those leaves there near the stem. And how the petals' prickly tips look just like the stubble I'm sure you'll grow one day. I'm kind of taken aback by how alike you two are now that I'm absorbing it all."

And the boy said, "Thanks, sir."

And the director said, "Thank you for coming, dear boy! And thank you for coming, sir!" And the director shook Chris's longest leaf heartily the way hearty men shake, and he tossed a potato sack to the boy, saying, "You should be able to share that okay," and then he was off to greet another duo.

After the racing, after the eating of potato salad and watermelon, after the frolicking with other children and their partners, such as somersaulting on soft grass and playing freeze tag among shade trees, after all that, the director let the boy keep his potato sack so that he could drag down the hill his father's pot and his blooming likeness, his second-place plaque and his three participant trophies, as well as an extra watermelon gifted to him by the woman who wagoned the watermelons up the hill that morning. When the land flattened out, the boy placed his goods into the burlap and humped them over his shoulder the rest of the way.

13

OUR BIRTHDAY WAS ON a Sunday. Ashley never said anything about it. But I knew it was coming up, and we had a date planned for Saturday. Saturday the 22nd of April—Eliot's cruelest month, the month of Chaucer's pilgrimaging, et cetera, et cetera—and at midnight we would both turn twenty-nine. And what was kind of neat about this is that we shared Shakespeare's birthday. April 23. He was born and maybe also died on that day. And I pictured people in the future reading Ashley's bio in the Norton and Longman and Bedford and Broadview anthologies and being all, Whoa, Ashley Farinha Smith and William Shakespeare shared a birthday.

But there were a few problems with the night-before-our-birthday date. For one, I was worried if I planned some big thing, she might be weirded out by it since she had no idea I knew. When I found out on our first date, I just figured she'd bring it up. But then when it started to get closer, I liked the idea of doing some surprise thing, something special since she's away from her family and oldest friends. And another problem was that I worried she'd still be creeped out by us sharing a birthday. I don't know why. I just worried about that. But the last thing I worried about is that Ashley sometimes conks out at eleven and I needed this girl to stay awake till midnight to surprise her.

So here was my surprise. I picked her up at 6:00 p.m., and I parked downtown. And we got a drink at a nice little café before dinner. We ordered café amarettos, which were great because they have espresso and brandy and something else sweet, so they're tasty but I was mainly glad Ashley was getting some caffeine in her. And I was wondering if she was going to bring up that tomorrow was her birthday, but so far she hadn't, and at this point, I didn't want her to because of the planning I'd done. After the café, we walked down Main Street and went into Mrs. Tiggy-Winkle's, a cute gift shop that sold all kinds of bizarre stuff. This wasn't on my agenda, but I thought it was a good idea. Ashley saw the place and said, "Hey, let's go in there." And I said, "Sure, why not?" And it was her first time, but my mom used to love to go there, so I'd been in here and there throughout my life, but I guess it had been a few years.

I bought Ashley a really nice framed print of the Cheshire Cat—not the Disney drawing but this really cool illustration from whoever the nineteenth-century artist was. The cat was gray and mostly normal-looking except for this massive grin. And he's sitting up in this stunning tree with these long winding branches with these bright green leaves, and I wanted nothing more than to own a house somewhere where grass grew without the aid of sprinklers, where Ashley and I could live together with that tree in our front yard, picnicking together in the shade when the weather was just right. Ashley was going to buy the print for herself, but I insisted and carried it around the shop for her. So then she walked around looking at things for me: coffee mugs in the shapes of different dog heads, hand-made soaps, a Jesus action figure, and she finally settled on a pair of socks. They had carrots on them. Tall green socks with orange dancing carrots, smiling and holding hands.

The clerk rang us up and said, "Special occasion?"

I said, "No, just a date." But then I added, "So, actually, yes. It's always a special occasion to be with her."

Outside the store along the walkway, water bubbled in a fountain, the streetlamps glowed orange, and tree trunks and branches gleamed with bright white lights wound around them. The night looked magical.

Ashley playfully hit me with the bag holding the socks. Then she pulled them out and placed them in my hands, saying, "You like socks, right?"

And I said, "Sure, of course."

And she smirked and said, "I thought so."

I slipped the socks into the bag with her Cheshire Cat print, and I tried to think of something clever to say, but nothing came to me, so I just said, "You ready for dinner?"

And she said, "Sounds good. Where to?"

I said, "Follow me." And I held out my arm, and she linked into it, and we walked side-by-side across the way to Las Campanas, the Mexican restaurant in one of the Mission Inn's outside patios. We were given a nice little table near a fire feature. Ashley sat closer to the flames because she got cold at night quicker than I did. Our waiter brought chips and salsa. Ashley ordered a margarita on the rocks, and I had a porter.

We sipped our drinks and caught up on our weeks. Work was work for both of us. She seemed less excited about her teaching and her students than she usually was, but the end of the academic year was nearby and I understood her being burnt out. I didn't get summers off at the café, of course, but my job was pretty stress-free compared to hers. And I asked about her pregnant sister-in-law too, and she said the pregnancy was going well. She said she was showing a little bit, had a small curve popping out, and I could tell she was really happy and a bit envious.

Then I ordered fish tacos and she ordered cheese enchiladas and I got another porter and she switched to red zin. Our waiter left us, and I said to Ashley, "Writing anything new?"

She said, "Yeah." She said, "I've been revising old poems to send to journals. And that process has sparked some new poems too. It's been great lately because I was in a bit of a slump."

She beamed happiness. "Awesome," I said. "I'm so thrilled for you," I said.

And she told me part of what got her going was getting copies of journals sent to her with her poems published in them. Seeing her name in print, seeing poems published she'd written years ago, that she'd spent hours writing, then trimming, then growing, scraping scraping scraping till they were just right— well, all of that was inspiring to her, so when three different journals that had published her poems arrived in her mailbox within a few days of each other, she reread her own poems and she read the other poems in the journals, and then she pulled out old notebooks and attended to old lines, and now she was excited for these words and lines given new lives, new shapes and sounds.

I said that was great. I was glad she'd been having some inspiration and good luck.

She said, "Knowing your craft is what matters. Inspiration isn't reliable."

And I said, "Oh, I'm sure you're right about that. For me, I wouldn't know because I tend to only write when I feel like it. If I don't feel like writing I just do something else. Didn't a poet say that once? He didn't write anything that wasn't a gift? Or something like that? That's like me. There's enough good writing in the world. I add to my notebooks when I feel moved to do so, but I'm not trying to force things out into a crowded market."

"And are you ready to show me some of this writing?" she said. "If you don't want any revision suggestions, I respect that. I'll just let you know which ones I like best. And I'll help you send them to journals and magazines if you like."

"Thanks," I said. "I'll print some out for you," I said.

We ate our food and chatted some more about this and that. Our writings came up again, her poems, my fictions and semi-poems, and the craziness that reality-TV-star Donald Trump had been president for three months, and the craziness of her getting used to California and people generally being rude without thinking they're being rude, and the craziness of getting older and feeling like the world has made living so much damn harder than it should be. Like, for example, why the hell do coupons exist? Just please make prices lower for all of us. And why do credit card APRs have to be so damn high, and if I'm getting so much useless mail and email at twenty-eight-almost-twenty-nine, just think of how miserable it will be in our thirties, forties, fifties, God willing, God willing, et cetera, et cetera.

And that last rant about the mail was hers, and she'd said the words "twenty-eight-almost-twenty-nine," and then she took a cheesy bite of enchilada, and then she swigged the last of her red and said, "Joe. Joe, it's my birthday tomorrow. No one out here knows that. I've been wanting to tell you. I should have told you."

"Wow," I said. "That's great." And I reached down for the bag with the Cheshire Cat print, and I pulled it out and said, "Happy birthday!"

And she laughed and spit enchilada out on me and said, "Shit! I'm so sorry."

I said, "No worries," and I tucked the print away, and I wiped my face, and then we had a third drink before paying and tipping and walking out arm-in-arm into the hotel lobby.

She asked where I was leading us, and I said the hotel was pretty amazing, that she'd appreciate its architecture and just walking around and looking at things in the hallways and staircases. And she said, "Can we do that?"

And I told her to follow me and pretend you belong. And we walked up the main staircase in the lobby and made it to the second floor, and I was right because she immediately was looking at the paintings on the walls and the desks and tables and bookshelves and other old wooden furniture on display behind velvet ropes. And we kept climbing the staircases and touring the hallways, and on the fourth floor the hallways are outside, and you can look down below to what I think is the hotel's Italian restaurant. And there were potted bougainvillea with their bright pink flowers stretching over the iron fencing, and outside the air was crisp, and down below people were drinking and laughing, and up above the sky was dark with bits of gray clouds, and there were orange lights in black sconces along the walls. And the walls held wooden doors with arched tops that led to some of the better rooms in the hotel. And we kept passing doors, and she was looking around at the loveliness of this hotel, and she was holding my hand, and then I stopped and took out a key and opened a door.

And she said, "What are you doing?"

And I swung the door open and clicked on a light and led her in. The room was full of balloons, and there were vases with yellow roses and pink roses and white roses, and there were red rose petals thrown all along the floor and bed, and there were three HAPPY BIRTHDAY signs drooping from corner to corner to corner to corner, and there was a bottle of champagne in an ice bucket that was pure ice earlier in the day but was now half water, half ice.

I shut the door, and she said, "Wow." She said, "When did you do this?" She said, "How did you know?"

"I got the room key at three and then I lugged everything up out of my car and spent a couple hours setting up before coming to get you." And she was looking around at everything, and I said, "I thought we could sleep here tonight. I don't expect anything. I just put the rose petals on the bed for decoration. I thought we could have champagne and put on a movie in bed. Then we can swim all day tomorrow and eat at the poolside. Celebrate our birthdays together with burgers and salads in the sun while dipping in and out of the jacuzzi. And they told me the pool is heated to eighty."

She turned her head away from the balloons and flowers and decorations and then she said, "It's your birthday too tomorrow?"

And I told her about how on our first date, when she was carded at dinner, I saw her birthday, and how I was going to blurt out something like, No way, we have the same birthday, but I said I really liked her and didn't want to weird her out or scare her off if she thought it was creepy or something. "So, anyway," I said. "Ever since then, I've been thinking about what to plan. I was going to keep us busy tonight until a few minutes before midnight, and then bring you up here and say, Surprise, right before the actual day, but—what time is it?—ten thirty—things didn't take as long as I thought with the café and restaurant and walking around the hotel, so I thought, Screw it; let's head up there now." And then I added, "I've got presents, too. Three of them, there on that table."

She looked at me real serious, eyes big, lips straight and touching.

And I said, "Are you okay? Is it okay that I did this? Do you want me to take you home?"

And she wrapped her arms around me and embraced me tighter than she ever has. And she said, "Thank you. It's all so wonderful." And she kissed me.

And I said, "Sure. Of course. Let's have at that champagne for a toast."

But she pulled out of my arms. And she walked backward. And she unbuttoned her shirt and set it on the edge of the bed. And she slipped off her shoes and socks and pants, and she was on the bed in her bra and underwear, sitting crisscross right in the center.

I said, "Are you sure? That's not why I did this."

And she said, "I know. And yes, I'm sure."

And that's all I needed, so I took off my shirt and pants but kept my boxers on to join her on the bed, and we got into a rhythm of kissing, and eventually our underwear was off too, and she asked me to dim the lights, so I did, and she wanted to be under the covers, so we were, and things moved wonderfully along.

Afterward, I had champagne, but she stuck with water, and I held her in bed and kissed her back and neck, and I asked her if she wanted to open her presents, but she said she'd like to wait until morning on the real day. And I said, "Sounds good," and she said, "Good night," and she fell asleep seconds after saying that because that's how she was.

It wasn't yet midnight, and I lay in bed with my hands behind my head while Ashley slept. I didn't want to watch TV or order a movie. I just looked at the ceiling and around the room, and I thought about those presents on the table in the corner. I hoped Ashley would think they were sweet when she opened them in the morning. I had it in mind to order room service, eggs and coffee and toast. And I'd watch Ashley open her gifts in the order I'd hand them to her. First the framed picture of Shakespeare with her face photoshopped over his. Then the thin cashmere sweater I'd gotten on sale at Nordstrom Rack. And last the silver necklace with a snowflake pendant that I'd had a jeweler special order three weeks ago.

The ceiling had tons of patterns to follow because the drywall was laid on thick with deep trowel marks. I think that's a real Spanish style. So my eyes followed the knife-like lines of the thick plaster, and I was still thinking about how and when and if I would ever tell Ashely about Cora. It seemed to me that Ashley was finally starting to fall for me. Not just because we'd had sex but because it was something I'd been feeling in the past week or two. When we started dating in February, I knew she was hesitant, and then in March I felt like we had a good thing but that it might just be temporary, that maybe I was just there because she didn't have anyone else. But things were changing. Things changed. We'd only been together two and a half months, but I could picture her now wanting a life for us together here in the Inland Empire.

14

MAY CAME, AND ON the first Saturday I picked up Ashley and we drove west to Huntington Beach. She wore a yellow sundress and had on the snowflake necklace I'd given her on the morning of our birthday two weeks ago. The drive took about an hour. It was a nice day, a hot one in Riverside but only in the 70s at the coast.

We ate an early lunch, and then we went walking in the sand like couples do, side-by-side, sometimes holding hands but she wasn't really a public-display-of-affection type. Not a cuddler either, and up until two weeks ago I thought she was a no-sex-until-marriage girl, or maybe a no-sex-until-engagement-ring girl, and I'd actually been saving up a bit for that, and thinking maybe in late summer I'd be far enough along in my courting to pop the question. But now because things had moved quicker between us—despite her pushing the pause button last weekend—I picked up a placeholder ring from an antique store yesterday. I'd like to propose with a proper diamond ring, but at the moment I was only able to afford something with a super-small stone, so instead of that I bought a silver ring with a little sea turtle on it. I wasn't planning on proposing today. I knew it was too soon. But I just wanted to have something on me just in case. Just in case there was a moment that seemed too good to pass up.

So we were walking in the sand like that, side-by-side, couple-like, and then we turned to face the ocean, and we were looking at the surfers out there. They were wearing wetsuits because the water was still cold even though the summer was coming, and we stood silently and watched them, and then Ashley said, "I'm moving back to the Midwest. In a week. I've taken a job in Minnesota."

I said, "Oh." I was floored, silent. Then I said, "What's the job?"

"One of the University of Minnesota campuses," she said. "Not the main one. It's in Duluth. The town's called Duluth."

I didn't know what to say next. I didn't know where I fell into all this. I was too caught-off-guard to be mad or scared exactly. But something in me was building. I said, "When did they call you up?"

She said, "Joe. Joseph. When I flew back for my friend's baby shower in February and also went to that conference. Well I also went up to Duluth for two days then. They're the ones who flew me out. I'd applied for some new jobs before we'd even met. When I got the campus invite from Duluth, I didn't tell you because we'd only been dating a short time. I wasn't sure if I'd get offered that job or any job, so I just didn't think it was important to tell you."

"No, I get it," I said. "It makes sense not to worry about it then."

"Thanks for understanding."

"So they just called you up? Are you excited?"

"They offered me the job a few days after I'd visited. It was back in February. I told them yes back then. It was actually the day you hit that guy on the bike."

"You've known since then?"

"Joe, I'm sorry. I just never felt the timing was right. This is a better job for me. Not as many classes. They actually want me to be writing. I was always going to take that job or any other like it. I'd move to Antarctica if it meant a better position. That's how it works in my line of work, okay? I was always going to take a better job if it came along. I didn't tell you about all of this because I wasn't sure where we were going. If we were going to fizzle out anyway, it wouldn't matter if I'd told you I was going to leave. I guess I thought that would happen with us. Then it became hard to tell you because I liked being around you and I didn't want you to get upset. And the night before my birthday. Our birthdays. I hadn't planned on doing that before. I'd only done that one other time. And that wasn't planned either. And I was too young. I haven't wanted to talk about any of this since then. I'm sorry I've been avoiding that conversation. About us being together. And I'm sorry I waited so long to tell you I've known for a while that I was going to move away. I like you. I like us together. I didn't want it to have to end too early. I should have followed through with that text I sent, but I wanted you to keep pursuing me."

I was silent now. I was mad now. No longer confused about my feelings. There they were, clear feelings, and I was pissed because I liked this girl and I thought she liked me. And she could have told me all this a long time ago.

I said, "I don't really know what to say to all of this. I thought things were going well."

"They were," she said. "They are. We can still have a nice week together."

I said, "Do you remember where I parked?"

She said, "Yeah?"

I took out my keys and handed them to her. I took out my cell phone and handed it to her. I took out my wallet, pulled out some bills and jammed them back in my pocket, and then handed her the wallet too. "You drive yourself home, okay," I said. "Do me a favor and put my cell and wallet in the glove compartment. And the keys too. Drive yourself home and leave the car by your place. Lock the keys inside. I have a spare. I'm going to take a cab home. I'll get the car later tonight. Can you drive yourself home, please?" I said. "Is that okay?" I said.

She said, "You're being silly." She said, "Come, let's go together and talk about this on the drive home." But she was already stuck holding my things, and I was off then. I was running into the ocean. I was in my shoes and pants and shirt. I was in the coolness. I was submerged. I was up. I was down. I was past the waves. I was swimming out and out, and there was nothing left on the beach for me to have to come back to. I was past the pier. And the water was heavy in my clothes, but I kept going, and then I turned to swim parallel to the shore. And if Ashley was watching me I might have looked like a seal bobbing up and down with my dark hair and shirt. If she was watching me I might have looked like some animal at home in the water, bobbing up and down while moving steadily along, appearing fluid and peaceful and in control.

But it didn't take long during this swim for my body to ache. And after maybe thirty minutes of swimming north along the coast, I had to make for the sand. When the waves helped carry me in, no one seemed to care about the madman who'd been swimming in his clothes. I walked out of the water like some sea creature coming to shore, my clothes sagging, my shoes like bricks, and I shuffled from sand to concrete, and I walked for a while until I gave up and plopped down on a bench. I sat staring out at the sea. I was cold. I was soaked through. But the sun was bright and the sky was clear. In time I'd be dry and this day would seem beautiful despite Ashley's news. I was in no rush. I took my shoes off and laid my socks out on the bench. I took my shirt off too and draped it behind me. And then I took out the wet bills and straightened them out too because I'd need them dry for cab fare or Uber or Lyft except I didn't have my phone. And when my fingers pulled out the bills, the silver ring with the little sea turtle clinked onto the bench. And for a half-second I thought about running to the sea and throwing the ring in, but that would be stupid. It was a nice ring, so I asked the sea turtle, "Did you have a nice swim?" and of course it was silent, but I still turned the ring a bit so the turtle could look toward the sand and water.

As soon as I was sun-dried and my skin was tight from the salt, I put on my shirt and socks and shoes and slipped the bills and ring back in my pocket. Then I walked a couple of blocks to a corner market and bought a water and had the clerk call me a cab.

XI

A Boy and His Owl

ONCE WHEN A BOY was a little, little boy, he couldn't sleep. In bed he listened to the live oak's branches scrape his third-story window. In bed he listened to the great horned owl nestle into the live oak's leaves and eat the Thompsons' cat. The great horned owl, which is also the tiger owl, which is also the hoot owl, pinned Oreo between branch and claw, then pierced the warm belly. The beak left the heart alone, and left the stomach alone, but searched out the liver in the center, needling fur and skin until an apple-sized opening let the liver slide out. Prize in claw, the great horned owl hurled the Thompsons' Oreo from his branch. And the cat kept her grace and corrected herself mid-flight so that she alighted on four paws, distributing her body's weight among all her legs even though she was lighter now.

But when the boy was a little, little boy, he lived in a one-story bungalow with Mom and Dad, and their only tree was a tangerine tree that yielded fruit with peels so loose even he could dig a nail in, slip finger under skin, and tear out the juicy flesh without calling for Mom's help. And when the boy was a little, little boy, he knew Dad meant it when he said their bed was off limits, that men—*son*—do not crawl into their parents' bed at night.

So once, then twice, then many times when he couldn't sleep because the pecking and slurping of the great horned owl kept him awake, he grabbed his blue blanket with orange basketballs and inched down the hallway toward his parents' room. Wrapped in his blanket, he curled into himself and slept on the hallway floor outside their closed door. In the morning, sometimes Dad would wake first and step over him on the way to get his coffee, but usually Mom opened the door first, and she'd scoop him up and return him to his bed while he pretended to be asleep.

Then after cereal, when he'd play outside and see Oreo stretching in the sun's warmth, he'd say, "I'm so sorry that keeps happening to you."

15

NINE DAYS WENT BY since Ashley broke the news that she was leaving, so she had certainly gone back to the Midwest already. I hadn't thought about it until I was riding back alone in the cab, but her school, Hardin College, the one she was leaving —it must have gotten out early for summer break since she was all wrapped up in early May. I didn't do much for the next few days. I'd gotten my car at 3:00 a.m. when I knew she'd be sleeping, and then I kept up with my work shifts and wondered if she'd pop in to apologize. But nothing. Then on this day, nine days after she dropped the news, I got a phone call from a number I didn't recognize, so I picked it up. I was hoping it was her. I was waiting for her to call. My feeling was that she needed to call me after what had happened.

I said, "Hello."

And someone said, "Hi, I'm a veterinary assistant at Magnolia Animal Hospital. Are you the owner of a mixed Blue Heeler?"

"A Blue Heeler?" I said. "No, no, that's not me." But then it all hit me, and I said, "Wait, is that a Cattle Dog? Do you have a gray herding dog there?"

"Yes, sir," she said. "He's here. It looks like he chewed through his rope. One of our clients found him wandering the streets and she drove him here to see if he had a microchip. Sir?" she said.

"Yeah."

"We are going to return this dog to you if you come pick him up, but we are going to ask you to let us explain proper care to you again. Okay?"

"I'm on my way," I said.

They grilled me pretty bad. The vet assistant and the lady who brought him in. She'd waited to get a look at me, to see what the guy looks like who ropes up his dog. They'd cut the rope off him because it was wrapped around his neck. They showed the rope to me, pointed out how rough it was, pointed out the chewed end and how much time and how much effort that would have taken. Then they dumped it in the trash. I said a friend had been watching him because I'd been working a lot lately. I said he was staying at a friend's house but I didn't know he'd been mistreating him. And the dog didn't look too good, it was true. His ribs popped out at the sides. His coat was mangy. But he was friendly and was happy to see me. They didn't seem to question whether or not the animal was mine since the microchip was linked to my cell number. I didn't know if Ronnie wasn't feeding him enough or if the dog just wasn't eating, but I knew I wasn't taking that dog back to him. Maybe Ronnie was dead, some boar's treasure. Maybe Ronnie was alive but this dog wanted out of the river. Either way, it didn't matter. Neither me nor this dog ever needed to see Ronnie again.

I left the vet's office with a new green collar and matching leash and a brush and a stainless-steel food bowl and water bowl and two big bags of expensive dog food. A hundred and fifty bucks total. I put the dog in the back seat, but as I was driving he crawled up to the front and sat in the passenger's seat. He sat there just like a person, on his ass with his back straight up, all proper looking.

"All right there, man," I said. "You think you're a person or something?"

At a stoplight, I pulled out my phone and found a different dog park to drive to. Before I took this dog to my apartment, I wanted to make sure he'd done his business and everything.

This other dog park was cleaner, had more grass but fewer shade trees. And no mountain or dry river or homeless camps. No long bridge and busy street. It was tucked away near a residential neighborhood. Real nice. No one else was there. It was late morning and most people would be at work. I was off that day. I had nothing to do but sit around and watch that dog get enjoyment from sniffing around everywhere, discovering newness all around him.

I brushed him after he plopped down to rest, and he already started looking better. I picked out loose hair and foxtails with the brush strokes and watched dust float off him too. We got back in the car. I'd put him in the back seat but he crawled up front again and sat there looking like a person. I started telling him about Ashley, just talking to him with the windows down as we meandered home, taking no route in particular. At some point in the drive, we passed a U-Haul place, and then I turned around at the next light and pulled into the lot and left the dog in the car with one window down a couple inches.

I went in and bought ten book boxes and ten medium-sized boxes and a roll of packer's tape to assemble them. I rented a trailer to drag behind my car too. Even had them put on a trailer hitch. I wanted to get a real small trailer, but they were out of the smallest one, so I had to rent this mid-sized one that was a little longer than my car. I could fit almost all my furniture in there, but my furniture was cheap and could be left behind, so I didn't yet know what I would load up and what I would leave behind. The stuff worth keeping could fit in, anyway.

In my apartment, I packed up boxes while the dog sniffed around. I didn't know what his name should be. I didn't know what Ronnie had been calling him, and I didn't care. This dog could learn a new name.

I texted Ashley, *I'm sorry for swimming off last week.* And then I kept packing. I knew she'd respond at some point. Maybe not till tonight. Maybe not till tomorrow. But she'd respond. I might say to her, People need to eat sandwiches in Duluth. I might say to her, That couch of yours is going to miss me if I don't tag along. And she might be charmed by my gesture to drive out there and find work and find my own place just so we could keep dating a while longer. She might be charmed by that, or maybe her mind had been made up all along. But I finished packing what I wanted. I spent the day hauling boxes into the trailer, loading up what I'd want for the next few weeks or months or years. I had all my books, and I dollied down my writing desk and my chair. My dresser was cheap, so I left it. At the last minute, I grabbed my old coffee table and the patio furniture I had in my living room. I left my old mattress and the bed frame. I left the microwave but took the coffee maker. I took all my clothes in trash bags. I wasn't planning on taking so much stuff, and when I was all done I'd cleared out almost everything. The trailer still had plenty of room since I'd packed things high. I thought that if I wanted to save money I could just sleep in the back instead of getting motel rooms.

I left without saying a word to anyone. I could call my landlord tomorrow or wait till I made it to Duluth, tell him my apartment's vacant and the leftover furniture's his if he wants it. And I could call my boss tomorrow, say, Sorry, say, It looks like you've lost your top sandwich man. And if there was anyone else worth calling, I could tell them all later too. That could wait. But tonight I was driving east and north. Tonight I was driving to see what state I would be in when Ashley finally texted, to see what route I was on then and if I needed to change my course or not.

But I was on the road for only a few hours before God stopped me. I'd typed *Duluth, MN* into my phone, and I was all set to drive through the night and the day and just stop every once in a while to let Ash out to stretch his legs and go to the bathroom. That's what I decided to call the dog, Ash, because he's the color of ash and it has a cool ring to it. And then it occurred to me that it sounded like an abbreviation for Ashley, and I figured she might be flattered by that, so I kept it for the drive, and then I figured we could change it later if she didn't like the name.

So when I typed in *Duluth, MN,* I saw a couple different routes I could take, and that was real exciting because I'd never driven through this great country, and I saw I'd get to go through Utah, which I'd seen a poster of before, Bryce Canyon, I think, pictures of rock formations—arches and pillars and whatnot—so I was excited about maybe passing through some beautiful nature like that, and I saw that I'd have to decide between Colorado and Wyoming, and that depending on which one I'd choose, I'd get to see either Nebraska or South Dakota, and man, I felt like following both routes if possible but was leaning toward Wyoming because I liked their license plates with the cowboy on the horse if I remembered correctly.

But anyway, I didn't even make it out of California. God stopped me in the middle of the Mojave Desert. Didn't even make it to Nevada, just drove about two and a half hours to the edge of California before I was stopped. It was dark, something like 2:00 am, and I'd just passed this tiny town called Baker. It was a trip because that town had this giant thermometer. Like a three- or four- or five-story-tall thermometer. And from a distance, I was all, What the heck's that thing? It looks like some laser shooting to heaven. And beside me, Ash was all, Let's go check it out. And I slowed down as we neared it, a pink neon tower with red and yellow numbers on the bottom half, and then I could make out that it was a thermometer, and it was telling me that it was 64 degrees, and there was even a glowing red sign that said, BAKER CA. GATEWAY TO DEATH VALLEY, and I was thinking, That's foreboding. And as I slowed by that giant thermometer, I counted its rung sections, the little ovals climbing to the sky that hold the temperature numbers, and the 64 was in an oval not even halfway up, and man oh man, I was wondering, Can it get to 120 or 130 during a summer day? Is that even possible on this planet? And who would be crazy enough to live near this ridiculous thermometer if that's how hot it can get? So I sped up away from the thing, and there were a few other lights in the town, lights from a Del Taco and a gas station, maybe a bar down the road, and I kept driving toward Ashley and Minnesota, and in my rear-view mirror I saw the lit-up thermometer growing smaller and shorter, its neon lights blurring into the night sky until it was gone.

Twenty or thirty minutes past Baker was where it happened. It was desolate. And dark. Nothing around again. Just highway and desert. Barely any light except moonlight and the rare headlights or brake lights. And then it happened somewhere between Baker and the Nevada state line. The terrain curved a bit, and a few small mountains popped up near the highway, and the wind was pushing against my car, so I just gripped the wheel firmly with both hands and kept driving forward. Ash had been sitting upright like a person like he does, but when the wind picked up and rocked the car, he got low and curled up in the passenger seat and looked like a dog again. I said, "It's okay, buddy, just some wind." He didn't respond, but I knew he'd be back up to his old self once the wind settled down. I kept driving, not thinking much of it, and then we approached another bend, and I was going fast because I was sure Ashley would want to continue our relationship once she saw I had moved for her. I just wanted to get to her. And I sped forward curving with the white line, and then when the road was straightening out again I could see these two eighteen-wheelers up ahead. The trucks were side-by-side, taking up the only two lanes, and they were still like thirty car lengths ahead of me, so I kept up my speed and waited for one of them to pass the other, but they stayed side-by-side, these long eighteen-wheelers, and the road was straight again, and then bam! just like that, the wind slammed into our sides, and my car was shoved over into the next lane before I straightened out again, but the trucks were done for. The trucks toppled like dominos. Their trailers absorbed that wind like a sail. When the first one tipped over, half its wheels were in the air for a long second, spinning forward but gripping nothing until the whole thing fell onto the second truck. Then the second one toppled from the weight of the first, and the driver tried to right the ship, I guess, but he made a real mess of it because as he turned, his whole trailer slid sideways.

I slammed on my brakes, of course, and poor Ash hit the glove compartment with his left shoulder, but he was fine. And I was able to stop my car before running into either truck or trailer, but the whole accident was a real disaster, a blockade. The trailers stretched out across both lanes and shoulders and it looked impossible for me to drive my car through. But I tried. I creeped up to each side to see if I could squeeze my car through because I was on a mission to get to Duluth. But it was no use. The road was blocked. So I got out to see if the drivers were okay.

One had a broken leg and one had a broken arm. Go figure. The one with the broken leg sat on the road near his truck. He'd called for an ambulance, which was on its way. I asked if I could help and he said, "Probably not." He'd just wait for the ambulance and try not to think about the pain. He was driving a Ralphs grocery truck. I thought maybe small talk would help. I asked him if he had any good produce in the back. He said, "What? I don't know," and then kept touching his bent leg where the bone popped out. I said I was going to go check on the other guy, told the broken-leg guy to holler if he wanted me to come back and check on him.

The guy with the broken arm was Sam. He had a name patch sewed to his shirt. He was driving a Mayflower moving truck, and he also said I probably couldn't do too much for him, that he would just wait for his ambulance since he'd also called one. The significance of him driving a moving truck then hit me. I wondered if it was Ashley's truck. If that was her life toppled over in that trailer. I said, "Sam, do you mind if I ask where you're heading? I mean where the truck's going." He said Denver. He said a nice young family was expecting to get their things delivered tomorrow evening. And then he said that at least they pack things well at Mayflower. At least they use a lot of bubble wrap and whatnot. Probably wouldn't be so bad after all.

While the drivers sat by their cabs, I went back to my car to check on Ash. As I said, he was fine. I turned on the car and reversed away from the wreckage, then idled for a few seconds. I turned on my headlights. Pretty soon an ambulance or two would show up. Maybe a firetruck. Then a ton of highway workers. Maybe a crane to right the trailers, not exactly sure. I could stay or I could go. It wouldn't matter. But I couldn't get through the mess for a while. There was no heading east for a while. And maybe it sounds naïve, but I got the sign. I got the message. God blocked that road. I wasn't meant to travel on. I was being protected. I wasn't supposed to pursue her. Because she hadn't texted back anyway. And she had planned on leaving me months ago. We were never going to be a thing. "We were never going to be a thing," I said. Then I said, "Thanks, God. Thanks for the clarity." I knew that if I sought out Ashley again something would stop me every time. It wouldn't always be two big rigs crashing and blocking my way. Maybe tomorrow a surprise heavy rain would cause boulders to slide down onto the road. Maybe on the third attempt an earthquake would split open the asphalt. I wasn't dense. I got the sign, and I didn't need to keep testing it. Once was enough.

I turned my car around and drove the wrong way down the highway, heading west. I drove until I could exit and drive safely on the proper side. Ash perked up again, sat tall, his back against the seatback, his legs dangling out in front of him. He said, Let's go check out that thermometer again. Let's go knock some trashcans over. Let's go get some food and then run around.

I said, "We can do that."

Ash nodded slightly and kept his gaze forward.

I said, "Tomorrow we can unpack these things and move back into my apartment."

Ash stayed quiet.

I said, "Or we can drive to Cora's and see if we can patch things up. She'd like this sea turtle on her right or left hand. And she'd like you. Maybe she'll want to throw her clothes and her fancy bed and her table and chairs into the other half of this trailer. Maybe she's ready to drive north to see her family, and we can take her there before continuing to Oregon. Or maybe she'll head somewhere east with us. Anywhere cold. Anywhere with real trees. No palm trees. I'm tired of palm trees."

I glanced to the right to see if Ash would offer any advice, but he just repeated himself, panting over and over, Let's go check out that thermometer again. Let's go knock some trashcans over. Let's go get some food and then run around.

I said, "Sounds good. Sounds good. Let's go run around tonight, and then when the sun comes up we'll knock on Cora's door and show her the space left for her in the trailer. We'll pack her up and head out where she tells us. We'll follow her. We'll follow her if she wants us to. We'll head out somewhere and never come back. And if she sees the space we have for her and examines her life and decides she wants to stay, we'll head north anyway. We'll drive north in the morning, then maybe east, because you need a crisp start like me, and we have our better things packed up and not enough good reasons to stay behind now that spring is fading and the summer's dog days are rushing toward this dried-up land."

XII

An Image

THEY SIT ON A front porch. They rock back and forth while the wood creaks beneath them. The air is not hot or cold and there is a breeze. They gaze out at a field that goes and goes. Animals are in the distance, perhaps cows, perhaps goats. The grass is electric green from all the rain, but now the sky is clear, and now the sun is just above that hill, either setting or rising while they rock and look outward.

16

HERE WAS OUR night in Baker:

I let Ash off his leash, and he stayed near me like a good boy. I told him he could run around like a madman but that he shouldn't stray too far.

He wagged his tail, saying, Of course. And then he proceeded to knock over one, two, then three trash cans. He dug through the debris, chewing up old taco wrappers, sniffing sniffing sniffing so much rancid goodness, and I trailed behind him, picking up the trash cans and putting back in what he didn't eat because I'm a good and thoughtful citizen.

Ash tired himself out. He was thirsty, tongue practically scraping the concrete as we walked. We entered Del Taco, and the kind elderly woman working gave me a bucket to fill up at the hose in the back. I ordered us two beef burritos and eight tacos.

I thanked the woman. I asked, "Do you get off soon?"

She said, "Five years if I'm lucky."

I said, "Sorry." I said, "I wish you were on your front porch tonight drinking tea, rocking back and forth and enjoying the cool evening."

"That was our plan, dear," she said. "That was our plan."

Out back, I filled the bucket with hose water and Ash slurped wildly, and we split the burritos and tacos, and then we had energy, and Ash barked, Let's run, and I said, "Sure," and we raced out into a field, Ash leading the way while I did my best to keep up. He headed for that giant thermometer lighting up the night sky. He sprinted, getting pretty far ahead of me, but I knew where he was going. When I finally made it out of the field and to the empty parking lot by the thermometer, Ash was running in circles around the thing, barking at the glowing neon interrupting the dark. I was panting. I fell to my knees. I thought I was in good shape since I liked to walk for miles and miles during my nighttime strolls, but this was different. My body ached. My lungs couldn't suck in enough air. I fell over, lying on the blacktop, stretching out my limbs so

I'd look like a starfish if anyone in heaven had been allowed to peer down at me in that moment.

Eventually, Ash tired out again and curled up beside me. We rested there for an hour or two or maybe more. I dreamed that I was a paralytic and spent every day outside on a cot in the desert. Every morning a woman with long brown hair down to her ankles would cover my body with a thick white blanket. She would do this after the sun had been in the sky for an hour or so, long enough for me to feel warmth on my face but before the sun would start to damage my useless limbs. Then she would lift a pitcher and pour water all over the white blanket and put a wet washcloth over my face. I would sleep like that during the day, and then before sunset, the long-haired woman would return and remove the blanket and washcloth, which had then just dried out. I would watch the end of the day and then stare out at the stars and night colors until the sun would rise and she'd return with the white blanket and washcloth and pitcher of water. I dreamed that I lived like this for years. I dreamed that I was as happy as anyone could be in the world. But when I woke up, I was really saddened by that existence, and I was relieved that my life wasn't really like that.

I sat up, and Ash perked up, and I stretched my stiff limbs, and Ash stretched his back upward, and the thermometer in Baker, California, read 61 degrees, and it was probably still an hour or two until sunrise.

We walked back to my car and the half-filled trailer, and I said to Ash, "Let's go check on Cora."

And he panted, Sounds good. I'd like to meet her.

So we drove back to Riverside. It took about two hours, and we were pretty quiet for most of the drive. Once or twice I almost drove off the road because my eyes were heavy, but when my car tires and the trailer tires hit those grooves at the edges—those grooves in the asphalt meant to wake you up, causing the vehicle and your whole body to vibrate like crazy—well that stirred me just right and helped get me to Cora's place safely. When I pulled up to Cora's apartment complex, it was still dark, so Ash and I waited in the car until the sun rose. I could tell it was going to be a beautiful day. It didn't take long for the morning gray to shift to blue, and the clouds were the wispy kinds that were formless, not like the kinds kids draw where the white and blue have strict boundaries, but the kind where you can't really see clouds except for some streaks of white just being hinted at through the blue behind it and in front of it.

I put Ash's leash on and told him he'd have to wear it here. We got out and he peed on a palm tree. Cora's door was right there. The blinds were closed. Was she alone in there? Was that Chad guy or someone else in there with her?

I didn't mind risking it. I didn't mind getting embarrassed by her if she told me no and wasn't interested in me crawling back to her. Ash's leash was in my right hand. With my left hand, I felt for the turtle ring in my pocket. I was going to give it to Cora whether or not she wanted me back. And I was about to walk up to her door and knock, but then a bike bell chimed in the street behind me, and I turned and expected to see a little kid riding around while chiming that little kid bike bell, but there was Ronnie, cruising down the street with his helmet on, ringing his bike bell, saying, "Wee. Wee." And he pointed to me as he rode by, and he stretched out his legs to each side like a little kid, and then kept peddling away.

I was floored. I said, "What the hell?" And Ash looked at me like, I don't know, man. What's that guy doing here?

So I got back in my car, and Ash and I drove off to follow Ronnie. He meandered through Cora's neighborhood. There was a library nearby. There was a convenience store. But he didn't seem to be going anywhere. He was just riding his bike up and down different residential streets. Not many people were out for the day yet. I followed slowly behind Ronnie, keeping my distance, and I knew I'd check in with Cora again in a bit. I was just super curious about what Ronnie was up to. But he was directionless. He was driven by some impulse that made sense only to him. But I told myself I'd follow him until he stopped somewhere, and then I'd decide if I should talk to him or just continue on with my life, and as I was thinking that, my phone buzzed, and a message from Ashley said, *I think I made a mistake. Can we talk?*

And I laughed. I was so happy to see her name pop up. But part of me wanted to reconnect with Cora, too. I was excited at the prospect of Cora. And I was angry with Ashley, but all the old desire and my infatuation with her rose to the surface, and I was brimming with a deep longing that I despised and loved. And then my car smacked into something, and a child's bike bell rang out, and for a second I thought, Oh my God, I hit a kid, but then I was relieved when I realized that I'd just hit Ronnie again.

I pulled over, and Ronnie was slowly getting up. He was gripping his ribs, hunched over.

He said, "What the fuck? Why'd you do that?"

I said, "It was an accident. Are you okay? Let me drive you somewhere."

A few people spilled out of their houses to see what the fuss was. Ronnie was sitting on the curb. His arms were scraped up, but nothing was swelling or broken. Someone had brought him a bottle of water. He sipped on it. I opened my trailer and put his bike inside. I told everyone I knew him and that I'd drive him to the hospital. They all seemed satisfied with that and went back into their homes.

Ronnie was still hunched over. I helped him up, and he leaned on me as we walked to my car. I opened a back door, and he crawled in and got himself into the fetal position. Ash stayed in the front sitting like a person. He didn't bother looking back at Ronnie. I started up the car and drove off. I said, "Ronnie. Ronnie, can you sit up?"

He just moaned.

I said, "Ronnie, do you want me to take you to the hospital?"

He said, "No." He said, "Just take me home. Jill will be waiting."

I drove to the Santa Ana River. I parked at the same entrance I used a few months ago when I visited his camp for the first time. I cracked Ash's window a couple inches and kept him in the car. He didn't need a reminder of the place where he used to be roped up. I helped Ronnie down the embankment and into his side of the dried-up river bottom. I told him I'd come back up for his bike, and he said, "What bike?"

We approached his burnt-orange tent, and he asked, "What's this place? I said take me home."

"This is your home," I said. And I unzipped the opening and helped him onto his pile of blankets. He curled into himself, hugging his knees. I said, "Can you straighten yourself out? Do you want to stretch out your legs?"

He groaned. He said, "Jill can help me when she gets home. You can go now. I'm going to rest like this. You can go now."

I thought about leaving him there. But I couldn't. Was it too late to get him back into my car and to the hospital? Should I call an ambulance? I said, "Ronnie, do you want me to call an ambulance? I don't think you're doing well."

He looked at me with a blank stare. He said, "Ace, you look so young. Did you shave?" And he coughed up some blood, and he lifted his shirt to wipe his mouth. And his stomach was a mixture of red and purple.

I pulled his shirt off and finished wiping his mouth. But then he spit up more blood. His body was burning up. None of his skin looked right. His stomach, chest, arms, everything was deep red or purple. He looked at me and said, "Jill can fix this." And then he winced, and he groaned, and it was clear he was in deep pain and there was no fixing his mind or body, and no help was coming, and he groaned and groaned while his body squirmed, and I held his hand while he gripped it, and with my free hand I took his bloodied shirt and brought it to his mouth, and at first I was going to wipe his mouth again, but he spit up more blood, and he cried out like a bear or lion that had been shot unfairly, and after he'd released his roar, I held down the shirt over his mouth, and I pinned him down with my elbow while smothering him with his bloodied shirt, and I did this out of instinct, and I wasn't surprised that I was doing this because he was going to die either way and all I could do was help speed along the process.

After his body quit shaking, I fell back into his blankets and released my own long scream. I screamed and screamed until I had no voice left. I crawled out of the tent, and the day was hot already, and I helped myself to a sip of Ronnie's water. In this moment, I knew Ash was safe in my car and that in a little while I'd hike back up to him and we'd drive away. And I wasn't yet thinking about whether I wanted to call Ashley and see if I could drive to Minnesota after all. Or if I wanted to surprise Cora and see if she'd take me back and travel somewhere else with me. I didn't decide those things until later. In this moment, I knew that I couldn't leave Ronnie like that. I drank another sip of water. I went back into the tent, and I removed Ronnie's clothes. I took him in my arms and stepped out of the tent like a groom carrying his bride. He was small in my arms, crumpled, his bearded cheek pressed against my heart, his legs and bare feet dangling from the bend of my right arm. I carried him to the trickle of water that is for reasons I will never know still called a river. I stretched out his body, and I took off my own shirt and soaked it in the clean water. I washed the blood from his face and then rinsed my shirt. Then I slicked back his hair and combed it with my fingers. After his face and hair, I cleaned the rest of his body. I washed his feet even though they weren't dirty. I picked him back up and stood there, the sun already working to dry us both.

I didn't have a shovel. I didn't want to lay him back in his bloodied tent. I didn't want to leave him exposed for the animals to feast on at night. I walked off with his clean body draped across my arms. I walked and didn't tire. I walked until I came across an indentation in the ground that looked large enough for his body. I placed him in the hole, but he didn't quite fit. I could have curled up his body and forced him inside, but his flesh was newly washed, and the skin would have been punctured by the hole's jagged edges. It didn't sit right with me to cram him inside and damage the body, so I tried to enlarge the hole with my hands and then a flat rock, but the earth refused to open. The ground was hard all around despite being next to running water. I picked up his body and walked farther down the river. I found more indentations, but his body was awkward in each one I tried. I walked and walked with his body dangling in my arms. His skin was warm against me, and then my arms grew numb, and I was afraid I would drop him, and I cried out, "Please, God, take him!" And my legs buckled at the next step, and my knees slammed into the rocky ground, but I didn't drop the body, and there before me was a hole much longer than the others I'd tried before. I laid Ronnie into the earthen grave. I stretched his body out and placed his arms across his chest. He fit perfectly. The hole must have been about six feet long and two feet wide. And it went about three feet down. Certainly, this hole had been prepared for him. I gathered pebbles first to fit around the shape of his body, and then I found enough small rocks to cover him gently. But there was still space above that layer, so I walked around collecting larger rocks so that no passerby could tell what vessel was buried there. At the end, my palms had little skin left, but I wouldn't notice that until after I'd journeyed back to my car and reached in my pocket for my keys, the quick pain returning my mind to its frail body. I'd built up Ronnie's grave until the ground was flat with layers of rock. I didn't think the animals could undo this.

Aknowledgments

Thanks to the editors of the following journals for first publishing these pieces:

Arkansas Review for an excerpt from Chapter 9 published as "At the Bottomland"

Blue Earth Review for "Once a Boy Woke Up in Sweat or Piss"

Fiction International for "Once a Dozen Strangers"

45th Parallel for "A Boy and His Father" and "A Boy and His Owl"

The Los Angeles Review for Chapter 11 published as "Aunt Liesel"

The MacGuffin for Chapter 7 and Appendix A and B published as "One Day at Work, With Appendix A: Recently Adopted Dog Lost Near Mt. Rubidoux, and Appendix B: At-Risk Missing Person with Alzheimer's"

The Normal School for "The Inspired Painting"

Notre Dame Review for "The Found Story of Guy Nielson, Last Saved 3/31/2017 10:14 p.m."

Pembroke Magazine for "A Boy and His Mother"

Quarter After Eight for "A Person and His Angel"

The Saturday Evening Post for an excerpt from Chapter 1 published as "A Play Called 'Companion'"

Thanks also to Gregory Wolfe for publishing this novel and for his care and attention throughout the process. Thanks to Tracy K. Smith for allowing my narrator to say aloud her fine poem "The Weather in Space." And thanks to Gilbert Allen, Bret Lott, and Gina Ochsner for taking the time to offer such generous blurbs.

Of course, as always, thanks to Elizabeth and our three daughters for filling my days with love and adventure. And thanks to so many family members, friends, colleagues, and students who have offered various forms of encouragement and enlightenment throughout the last few years of tackling this novel.

Quotation Credits

Chapter 4:

Tracy K. Smith, excerpts from "The Weather in Space" from *Such Color: New and Selected Poems*. Copyright © 2011 by Tracy K. Smith. Reprinted with the permission of The Permissions Company, LLC on behalf of Graywolf Press, Minneapolis, Minnesota, www.graywolfpress.org.

IX [The Cora Fragment]:

The Vulgate Bible. Vol. III. The Poetical Books. Douay-Rheims Translation. Edited by Swift Edgar with Angela M. Kinney. Dumbarton Oaks Medieval Library. Harvard University Press, 2011.

Latin text only. Cora's English translations are by Derek Updegraff.

This book was set in Adobe Jenson, named after the fifteenth century French engraver, printer, and type designer, Nicholas Jenson. His typefaces were strongly influenced by scripts employed by the Renaissance humanists, who were in turn inspired by what they had discovered on ancient Roman monuments.

This book was designed by Shannon Carter, Ian Creeger, and Gregory Wolfe. It was published in hardcover, paperback, and electronic formats by Slant Books, Seattle, Washington.

Cover photo by Nicolò Bettoni on Unsplash.